MERAN'S REPROACH

BOOK TWO

LEGEND OF THE ANCIENTS

THE BOOKS OF LOCURNIA

DEONNE DANE

Published by Black Onyx Publishing

Copyright © 2020 by Deonne Dane

ISBN: 978-0-473-54541-3 (Kindle Edition)

ISBN: 978-0-473-54540-6 (EPUB)

ISBN: 978-0-473-54539-0 (paperback)

Cover Image by: B King

Edited by: Emma Bryson

*Meran's Reproach is the second book in the Legend of the Ancients series. The books of Locurnia contain explicit material and are intended for mature adults 18 and over.

To Grace for all her encouragement and enthusiasm

LOCURNIA
Port City of Dun

CHAPTER ONE

The hunt had been a success, Meran's kill now hanging in the cool storeroom. He and his friends were but a few steps from making their escape from the Durante's estate when exasperated words froze them in their tracks.

"Where have you been?"

Caught! And so quickly, gods damn! What ill-luck.

"Patrice?" Meran turned towards the woman hastening in their direction, her cloak billowing, the fine silk of her gown fluttering about her slim legs as she crossed the villa's inner courtyard.

His sister's cheeks shone with a rosy tint, and strands of her fair hair flowed free from the loose knot she had fashioned at the back of her head; her normally stoic presence replaced by a clenched jaw and lips taut with agitation.

Somewhere between the butchery's storeroom, the wet room, and the back of the bakehouse, she must have spied them. Meran had hoped to remain unseen by those in the main house as he and the hunting party slipped through one of the many shops lining the rear of his father's estate. But he and his two boisterous companions had been none too quiet, the furore of their day's successes prominent in their laughter and loud conversation.

Meran swallowed his annoyance and stepped out from the shaded doorway, every good feeling ebbing away. This promised to be a conversation better had away from the ears of his father's tenants. He made to join her.

The shriek of the youngest Durante, coming from within the depths of the bakery, interrupted his intention. "Merry, Merry!" He heard the crash of a stool and, like a meteor streaking past his two startled friends, a little girl hurtled towards him, arms grasping about his thighs with a firm, excited clasp.

A cloud of flour wafted from her dress, adding to the blood and grime already spattered over his britches. "Sofie," he said, trying to ignore the storm gathering behind Patrice's hazel gaze as she surveyed their greeting. At least someone was glad to see him. Meran returned his young sister's affection as best he could without making her more dishevelled. "Have you been playing baker?"

"Yes." Sofie grinned, a delighted sparkle glinting in her coppery eyes. "I have been rollering, and patting, and cutting grooves in the baker's bread."

"You two, do not think to distract me," Patrice said, her impatience ripe, though she unwound Sofie's clasp from his clothing with nought but a gentle insistence. Annoyed slaps, however, dusted the little girl's doughy handprints off his britches. "Where have the lot of you been skiving off to?"

"I should think it obvious," Meran said, sweeping a hand to indicate the state of his clothes.

Thunder rolled across Patrice's fair brow. "You will not take that tone with me. Father is a bear with a sore head. He had more than one visitor yester eve and you were not to be found. His rage is still incandescent."

Although he could not bring himself to feel sorry on his father's behalf, Meran did have the decency to hold back any further insolence.

A streak of concern softened the accusation in Patrice's eyes.

Meran sighed, sure that, unlike his sister's, his father's concern had not been for his safety. Durans Durante no doubt fumed that Meran had used his new-found freedom at the university's halls of residence to pursue his own interests rather than to align them with his father's wishes. It made Meran more determined to have his way. After all, a man should forge his own destiny.

The tell-tale silence from the bakery's kitchen alerted him to the occupants' curiosity, the sudden weight of it reminding him that this was not a conversation to be had in their hearing. Nor should it be had in front of his friends, either. He turned to take in the discomfort on Ellom's face, though it came laced with sympathy. Ormand, on the other hand, effected an artless expression that all serving men, it seemed, had perfected.

Their appearances, along with his, were rumpled and stained. Water still dripped from the cuffs of their britches after the washing they had given their caked boots in the estate's wet room. Meran felt the forest grime and the sweat of his labours itching on his skin. He had considered it a satisfactory consequence of his efforts, but his father's apparent displeasure took all the joy from the success of the hunt. A deer, and downed by his own arrow, no less.

"Lads," Meran lowered his voice. "Seems there is a to-do brewing to which I must tend. I will meet you once this is all sorted. Say, Ramon's Bathhouse in a half turn of the dial?"

Both offered him questioning scrutiny. Ramon's was one of the port city's better establishments, yet nothing compared to the bathing rooms in his father's villa. But the walls of the main house had ears. Meran knew he would need to speak freely after his pending interview, if for nothing more than to relieve his pent feelings.

As if realising his intention the young men nodded almost in unison, and after, somewhat unfairly, offering Patrice a wary glance, they retreated. Truly, his sister could be formidable. The household ran to perfection under her direction. But beneath her stoic exterior, Meran knew there lurked a malleable heart.

Albeit one that was not so evident in this moment.

Meran turned back to the slim blonde, her delicate jaw taut with exasperation, and guided both siblings from the curious ears of the baker and his assistants. "I assure, I left word with the custodian at the halls should anyone need to know," he said, leading them out into the cooling breeze that flustered about the villa's inner courtyard. "I cannot be blamed if none thought to consult him." Still, a couple of days spent in the woods with friends had meant some of his obligations had fallen by the wayside. "Did Thoran tell Father that I missed a lecture? It was just the one and nothing I cannot catch up on."

"Father expects you to miss none," Patrice said, the curves of her striking face softening from the glare of her previous admonishment. Idly, she retrieved a kerchief from her sleeve and began to wipe Sofie's hands. The little girl submitted in silence to the vigorous strokes. "Even I know of Master Thoran's penchant to take the liveliest of tale and make it unutterably miserable," Patrice raised the cloth in her clenched fist, "but what were you thinking? You cannot throw your studies aside on a mere whim."

"I had my reasons," Meran answered. Distraction, foremost.

"And are they sufficient to appease our father?"

Meran scowled. Nothing would be adequate for that, and he knew it. Had known it even though he had talked himself into the outing. The plausibility of his excuses had seemed valid at the time: fresh meat was always a welcome commodity at the tenant's butchery, or even for the Durante's kitchen... Ellom had requested his company... Ormand had accompanied him to ensure his safety... he would increase the much-needed skill of the bow with the practice... it was one day's worth of tedious lectures and tutorials, what would it hurt to miss them?

But the distraction had proven a dismal failure. The dream had still returned. Despite his friends' presence, despite the exhaustion that had claimed his body during the adventure. Like a ceaseless wraith, it had slipped from the dreamlands to torment him.

It had taken every drop of willpower to hide his distress from his companions before the current day's activity had done its work. For a time, he had slipped into a modicum of peace.

That peace was now well shattered.

"From that look on your face, I can see they are not." Patrice sighed, shaking her head in resignation. "What is to be done with you? You do not realise that it is not you alone that suffers—"

"Oh, here," Meran interrupted. "I know you would prefer not to be the one who must smooth our sire's ruffled feathers, but you are so good at it."

Her hazel eyes met his with rueful reproach. "I would not have to do it if you but tried to meet his expectations. You are the—"

"His expectations are impossible," he cut her short. She had been about to say, *heir*. Meran did not want to hear it. Durans Durante's demands of his heir were not impossible—at least not for a man with unquestioning loyalty to the Durante name, the charisma to lead, and an unflagging drive for perfection; but they were impossible for Meran. Not because he lacked those qualities, but because he could not fit the role to the degree that would ever satisfy his father.

As if to distract him from his self-pity, small arms wrapped about one of his legs, a warm cheek pressing into his hip as Sofie hugged him tight. "Poor, poor Merry," she said. Despite himself, he smiled. The child could not understand, still, her sympathy soothed the jagged edge of the wounds that sprang to life with the remembrance of the man his sire preferred.

"I think you do both yourself and others a disservice," Patrice said.

"Oh, lords, how?" How could his behaviour impinge on anyone? Except for his father. Durans Durante ignored his servants' wellbeing in favour of Patrice's oversight. He submitted to his betters even before the regime had changed after the Serpent War, and he kept friends at arm's length as if he feared their undue influence. There were but a few pleasures his father allowed himself.

"He had word from the temple, from the *Summus Sanctus* after Master Thoran took his leave," Patrice answered, her face sombre. "A petition against your friend, against his exhibition at the Civilus. They will not have a lord marshal support such a culture of hedonism. They forbid father's patronage for Jon on the grounds of indecency."

"By the gods! What nonsense is this?" Jon Reko's exhibition at the Civilus Gallery had been touted as an unmitigated success. The Port City of Dun had been all atwitter for days thereafter at the wonder and decadence of it all. "Provocative or not, his work is art. Father will not stand for such obstruction."

"He was already incensed by Thoran's revelation," she answered with equal exasperation. "It did not put him in the best disposition. He has said he will not fight it. A missive has already been sent to your friend, withdrawing his promised assistance."

"No!" It was unthinkable. How could his father consider such a thing? Lord Marshal Durans had always been a connoisseur of the arts. Paintings, sculptures, and glasswork adorned the floor and walls of the Durantes' sprawling villa, while unique pieces of jewellery filled many a chest and trinket box.

But Meran had no doubt that his father had been furious at his absconding. The damning rush of enlightenment forced its way into Meran's reality. "Does he think to punish me by punishing my friend? This is preposterous! His pique cannot be allowed to destroy Jon's livelihood."

A light patting against his thigh intruded on the flames of anger urging him to confront the man he had hoped to avoid for as long as possible; the injustice of it all forcing his hand.

"Never fear, Merry," Sofie said. "Jon will still make your stone man."

"Pray, what?"

"Hush," Patrice skimmed a caress over Sofie's fiery hair and disentangled the child from Meran's leg, as if afraid she might be caught in his haste to confront their father. "It is not the time for that now," she said gently.

Sofie's blushing lips quivered for a moment and she buried her face in Patrice's skirts. Meran's heart pricked at her dejection. But her words sent confusion flustering through his chest and threading through the turmoil that already tore at him—that she knew of Jon's talent for sculpting came as a surprise. Yet, that was the way of small children.

This he knew from his own experience. As a youngster, he had tailed both his father and older brother. Like a shadow, he had picked up titbits of gossip. Knowledge that made him feel important, included, even if he were not.

But if Jon lost their sire's patronage because of him, Sofie's innocent reassurances were unlikely to ever come true. Meran turned from the pair and headed with determined, angry strides across the courtyard to the sprawling structure that had been his home for as long as he could remember. His own contentions with his sire all but forgot at Jon's injustice. He could not allow that decision to stand.

CHAPTER TWO

Durans Durante did not turn from his contemplation of the flames in the large fireplace as Meran stormed into his father's private room.

"Well, finally, the prodigal deigns to return," his father said, the sneer redolent in his voice.

Meran's cheeks heated, "We need to talk," he said, his chest tightening as he struggled not to let his father's mere presence kill off the passion of his protest. "I was gone but one night," he accused, sweeping his supposed misdemeanour beneath the rug. "And in that time, I hear you think to ruin a man's future."

Meran watched his sire's broad back tense beneath the fabric of his heavily embroidered housecoat.

The lord marshal turned, offering Meran a baleful, brilliant blue glare. "Your friends, what are they to me? This family and your place in it, that is my priority."

"What has that to do with aught?" Meran asked. "Must I remind you that it was you who set Jon on his course? And at the first sign of opposition, you abandon him."

His father grunted as if something pained him. No doubt his hypocrisy was giving him indigestion. *Good.* But it did not stop fury boiling behind his taut expression. "And may I remind you," his father's lips pinched with the effort to contain himself, "that this is not about Jon, it is about you and your apathy. It is about your continued disdain for authority. Master Thoran is at his wits' end."

Exasperation erupted, Meran's voice scaling higher. "It was one lecture—"

His father cut him short. "It is about your future. How will you ever amount to anything if you do not take your studies or your duties seriously?"

"And you think to force my hand by punishing a man who is my friend? A man in need of your support," Meran could feel the snare stretch his lips, "because such action will bend me to your will?"

"Why must you forever kick against the pricks?" Lord Marshal Durans waved a rolled scroll in Meran's direction as if to emphasize his argument. "This is from the temple, the *Summus Sanctus*—"

"Patrice has said," Meran interrupted. It was no more than an excuse for his sire's retaliation.

The glass of wine in his father's other hand almost spilled beneath his tightening grip. "Then tell me, boy. In your infinite wisdom, how may I keep the peace when the priest threatens riots from his assembly? As lord marshal of this burg, I must pour oil on troubled waters, not stir them by pandering to my son's whims and those of his dissolute friends."

"So now you sacrifice Jon's future on the altar of the unwashed for nothing more than your pique?"

"You will not be impertinent," his father replied.

"Pray, why? You know Jon worked his fingers to the bone to get his pieces ready in time for that spectacle. A spectacle you were only too eager to back."

His father downed his drink in one gulp and turned back to the mantelpiece in a gesture much like dismissal. Dismissal of his part in what Meran could only see as the betrayal of his friend. A friend, Meran had recently considered, his father preferred more than his own son. A change of subject brewed behind his father's eyes, words fomenting behind those lips to lambast him into submission. Meran determined he would not allow that to happen.

Yet, how to get through to the obstinate man? Rubbing a frustrated hand across his face, Meran attempted a different tack. "You have a duty to your word, father. No matter the consequence, a promise has been made. You are a lord marshal; your word is your bond."

"Oh, that it is." His father threw a withering glance over his shoulder. "Do not think to constrain me with words to induce my repentance. My oaths were given to the Primoris to keep the peace of Dun and its surrounds, no matter my feeling."

"But why should the muttering of the priggish and self-righteous outweigh the promise of a man his livelihood?" Could his father not see the inequity? His was no more valid an excuse than using it to chastise Meran for what the man considered self-indulgent behaviour.

Meran did not get his answer. "Enough," his father shouted. Eyes closed, he raised his fists, the parchment crumpling. "Your whining is like a wasp at my buttock. The decision is made, and I will have no more of it. When will you learn to obey my word?"

"When you keep it," Meran answered, his temper flaring as he towered over his father, bending as if to place himself nose to nose.

Durans Durante showed no fear. Leaning in, his finger tapped with the force of a punch into Meran's chest. "If an oath is so indisputable, what of yours, boy?" And thus, the man brought the conversation back to the topic of his greatest interest.

Meran reeled back at his vehemence. "I have sworn nothing." At least, nought that he could think of. Meran forbade himself from swearing any words that could be used to bind him.

"You signed a promissory with the executor of your mother's estate that you would use her funds in the pursuit of your education." Glee echoed in his father's damning words.

Meran's heart sank. Of course he had. At the time, nothing had been more important than the opportunity to flee the feelings of inadequacy that came from living beneath his sire's roof. "It pays for my lodgings at the university and the cost of my learning, nothing more."

"You made an oath to the dean that you would complete your studies with all care and conscientiousness. Is that not part of the deed between yourself, the university and those that deign to sponsor you?"

"It was simply a requirement of entrance, by the gods!" How could this be held against him? All the student body had to comply or be denied acceptance. And now none but he was being held to its letter— an unfair expectation when revelries and debauches abounded both on and off campus. "It was but one day, for the pity's sake." One day in which he had thought to leave his cares behind. Was he not even allowed that small a concession?

"I am your father, your primary benefactor. By proxy, you made the oath to me and you will fulfil it, or by the gods, I will separate you from any that dare to distract you from your calling. I care little who they might be, nor who I may offend."

Meran's back snapped upright, rigid.

His calling?

Impossible!

"I've had but one vision. One, father, at the time of my change. Your hopes that I will ever gain this magic are futile." Nine years from that moment and Meran had not been transformed. He had witnessed nothing new, only the same torturous insight, over and over. No amount of pining could move him from that fearful place. "I am not who you think me. Not who you declare me to be and no amount of learning will ever make me so."

"You are a Durante," his father said. "You are my blood. A Durante does not give up; does not fail in his purpose, nor does he run from it." His lips drew back into a snarl of despite. "But you? Your eyes ever fall from your prize. You are just as your mother, flitting from one fancy to another. Well—I will not have that in my heir." The man's eyelids snapped shut as if he could not bear to look at Meran. "By the gods! I rue the day a blade bled all the loyalty and wit from this family. Now I am left with nought but girls and nonsense."

Nonsense? Pain whiplashed through Meran's heart, a buzzing ringing in his ears as if all the blood had drained from his head and sat, an unpurgeable constriction in his chest.

"I had nought to do with what happened to Beorn." Meran's words crackled beneath a surge of devastation. He had been all of seven when the Serpent War came to its end. "I never wanted this. I never wanted to take his place, never wanted to be him."

His father's lips curled into a sneer. "You could never. To him, you do not hold a candle."

The magnitude of the wound Durans Durante's declaration dealt left Meran speechless. He turned on his heels. It was not cowardice, though his father might proclaim it so, but self-preservation. He had no further use for this conversation.

Striding from the small sitting room into the late afternoon gloom of the villa's atrium, his reflection caught in the stunning wall of glassed mosaic; his image fractured and crazed, just as his emotions. He could not bear to see himself compared to Beorn. They were too different.

Oh, Meran had always been touted as unique, even beautiful. A man of great height, he possessed a lithe physique and a rich golden tan. His hair fell in long silvery-white waves and his eyes were a startling blue. Some boasted he had a face that could charm the masses, but in comparison to his brother his presence was deemed callow. Beorn had been everything a lord marshal could have ever hoped for in his firstborn. A natural-born leader, filled with charisma.

"Where do you head to?" Patrice called.

How much had she heard? Did he detect pity? Meran barely slowed as he raced past.

"Meran?"

"I am in no mood for chatter," he called back, his only plan to wallow in his own misery and failure.

"Brother!"

Patrice's sharp tone pulled him up short. She deserved better than for him to be so ill-mannered. For all her reprimands, he could always rely upon her to forgive him any indiscretion. He had no excuse for his rudeness.

"I promised to meet the lads at the baths. There is a sudden stench of incivility that hangs over me of late, that I must get rid of."

Patrice's sigh of resignation followed him as he strode for the door without a backward glance.

Save for a few patrons, Ramon's appeared to be empty when Meran arrived. It was unlikely to fill until its normal clientele, merchants mostly, had finished with their day. Meran discarded his clothes in the changing room and then submitted to the administration of an attendant. Slathered in a fine oil fragranced with hints of forests thick with crushed pine needles, he let much of his pique slide away.

Frustration and obligation scraped free with every deft stroke of the attendant's wooden spatula. His father's damning words and the knowledge of his mediocrity in the man's eyes, he allowed to slip away along with the sweat and the grime. Away from Durans Durante's presence, Meran let the weight of his burdens lift and float free.

All but the one: how to fix Jon's perilous strait. As the ultimate cause of the situation his friend now found himself in, it was his duty.

Meran had funds, of course, but none that did not carry obligation. His father kept him clothed and fed, and his mother's estate provided a roof over his head. But neither the executors nor his sire would allow its use on a man who had incurred the wrath of the high priest, no matter how generous Meran wished to be.

And while not meagre, his allowances would not stretch to cover the hire of a workspace and lodgings; nor would it pay for the food and the amenities of life required for the two or three years Jon would need to create a further masterpiece. No, Meran would have to secure Jon another patron. One who did not care for the *Summus Sanctus'* good opinion.

And that could prove impossible.

"All finished, sir," the attendant indicated with a small bow as he stepped back, rousing Meran from the depths of his contemplations.

"My thanks," he said, looking around for the other lads. Spying Ellom sitting alone at the far end of the central pool amidst a shimmer of steam, he made his way around the tiled edge. "Is Ormand from here already? I had not thought I had been so long." The warmth bit at his tender scrapes as Meran lowered himself onto the submerged ledge beside the smaller man. He let out a low hiss until the heat sank in and he sighed with relief.

"He had another commitment," Ellom replied, his smile relieved as if he had wondered if Meran would turn up to keep him company. "Somewhat to do with a chore his father had insisted upon."

"Ah. A serving man's fate, to always be at the beck and call of others." Not too much different from a son to his father, Meran brooded. He did not know how Ormand managed to effect such stoicism in the face of it.

"Well, so how went it?" Ellom asked once Meran settled himself, the water rising to lap beneath his pits.

"Do not ask."

"That bad, eh?"

"It was an interview best forgot." Still, Meran let out an exasperated expletive. "I swear on my life, I will never be like him. People are never things to be used or cast aside."

"You should have said if your joining the hunt would cause such a ruckus. We could have delayed it," Ellom offered, then laughed at the incredulous look on Meran's face. "Or not. But, we could have at the least taken the spoils to my family's estate."

"It was my kill." It did not seem right to Meran to hunt for the benefit of others when the Durante's own tenants were in equal need. "Besides, I had not thought Patrice would be so vigilant. Although, I guess it could have been ill-luck that I chose the bakehouse as our means of escape on a day when Sofie played at being baker."

Ellom nodded, curiosity brightening his grey eyes. "I am surprised that your father would approve of a Durante having such a fellowship with his tenants."

"That is Patrice's doing." Meran brushed it off. "Besides, I'm not sure he cares enough to voice his opinion on the matter." His father took little note of the women in his household. Only the honour of the Durante name seemed to matter to the man, and Meran's sisters would be beholden to the name of whomever they ended up betrothed to.

Ellom's fair brows met the high sweep of his bangs.

"My sister declares that if the raising of Sofie falls to her lot, it will be done in a manner she sees fit. She'll let none tell her otherwise," Meran said. "And that goes for our sire. I admit, very little is denied the child and yet it has failed to forge even one self-centred bone in her body."

Ellom laughed. "Early days yet. She is what; barely six years? The twins were sweet girls too until they reached their change. Honestly, their magic came in, along with their budding womanhood, and they turned into veritable vixens."

Meran smiled. Ellom's younger sisters were a handful, to be sure. They were one of the reasons Meran had stopped going to the Marius' estate to meet up with Ellom. The lasses took an inordinate amount of interest in him, which no matter their wishes, he could not return.

"Where are we going after this?" Ellom asked as they rose from the pool, water streaming the lines of their bodies to puddle at their feet and run down the grooves of the tiles.

Meran shrugged, now uncertain of his feelings. "I had not thought." His troubles returned to taunt him. The night loomed, ominous. He would have to sleep, and with sleep came the potential terror of the vision's return. With that possibility, his father's demands crashed over him. The man wanted something Meran could not give. The prestige of proclaiming a Durante a true seer. It wasn't as if Meran did not want to—the potential was there, he just could not wield that power.

They made it to the changing room. After a perfunctory wipe down, Meran began to pull his soiled clothing back on. "To get a fresh change of clothes would undoubtedly please me," Meran said, nose goaded by the stale smell.

"I heard Jon say the lads are gathering at the Hornet's Nest," Ellom said, dressed in a clean tunic and breeches, he had the sense to bring in his pack.

He did not quite remember where, but Meran seemed to have lost his own pack to the events of the afternoon. Probably dropped in his haste in the Durante's courtyard.

"We could go there after," Ellom suggested.

Meran sighed. His troubles loomed like oppressive fog; his way unclear, but until he found a solution to Jon's situation, fraternizing with the man felt too confronting. "I find I am not of a mind. Sadly, my tête-à-tête with Father has left me somewhat unsociable."

"Shall we head to mine?" Ellom asked. "The summer house is free. You need not meet up with the diabolical duet that is my sisters…"

"That is something, at least." Meran replied with a wry smile. Still, he would have to enter into pleasantries with Mistress Marius. A woman he well liked from the years of visiting he had done through the long friendship he had held with her son. "I don't know. Your mother deserves more than my dour company, and I feel barely fit for yours let alone your dam's."

"Perhaps a little of *this* will relieve your feelings." Ellom delved into the pouch he had affixed to his belt. Pulling free a small bag and pipe, he waggled it before Meran's eyes, smiling slyly. "Hampr. I had thought to take it to the gathering. An anticipatory celebration. Plans are moving along nicely within the history faculty, and finally I feel that I am getting somewhere."

"Are you sure you are not being premature?" Failure and disappointment were often the consequences of rushing in ill-prepared.

Ellom shrugged. "Mayhap. We shall see. But there is no reason that we may not indulge in a puff or two by ourselves."

Oh, there was a significant reason why Meran should not partake. The veil between reality and the dreamland could be weakened under its influence. But still, he nodded his agreement.

A mulish and contrary feeling overwhelmed him; a fist shake at his fate. It was possible that the consequence was not inevitable. Ellom's company could prove the distraction he needed, and his woes would at least be numbed by the hampr's effect. It was a chance he could take.

"Come on," he said. "There are good stone walls at my lodgings, better than your summer house at least."

With their course decided, they made all haste to the rows of apartment buildings at the back of the university. Soon they were striding beneath the rough-hewn whitewashed arches and down the corridor to the doors of Meran's rooms. Flinging them open, Meran entered a tidy entrance hall that led to an atrium beyond. To one side was a separate sitting room; to the other, a sleeping chamber complete with anteroom.

Ellom threw himself down on the brocade-covered daybed,

plumping the cushions and adjusting the fur throw beneath his seat. Meran trailed the line of rugs strewn over the cool tiles until he reached a row of windows. He threw back the shutters, letting in the last of the evening light.

"Is that one of Jon's?" Ellom eyed a gilt-edged framed painting of a pair mid-fellatio.

Meran turned from his course, tunic caught on his shoulders as he made to pull it off. "What do you think?"

"I think it is a fine likeness of Ormand's posterior."

"How do you know it is Ormand? You can't see his face." Meran tossed the dirty tunic at his friend with a suggestive leer. Of course, Ellom had guessed aright. And the other figure, with silvery-white locks partially obscuring the face as it looked at the man at his feet, was no doubt meant to be him. Not that Jon had painted the pair of them in the midst of a rut. Though it most likely represented a composition cobbled together from Jon's observations at the celebrations Meran had thrown in these very rooms.

Ellom laughed and flicked the tunic to the floor. "I don't recall seeing this one at the Civilus."

Meran made a rude noise. "If the high priest and his followers took umbrage at what was on display there, imagine what fuss they would make of a piece such as this. Even Jon judged this as not one of his more... tasteful."

"But you like it, though?" Ellom posed the question as more a statement.

Meran smiled again, casting the painting a considering glance. More suggestive than lewd, despite the subject matter, Jon had managed to make it about form, energy, and beauty. Still, he tossed Ellom a wink. "I have always been rather fond of Ormand's... attributes." That was not to say he did not enjoy other people's attributes equally, but Ormand was undeniably a very finely-crafted specimen.

"Oh, off with you," Ellom pulled his pouch free. "And while you change, I shall ready the pipe."

Deep into the evening, they shared long, slow drags of the hampr and eased back into the luxury of Meran's daybed to enjoy relaxed conversation. Contentment swirled in Meran's chest as the chatter turned to an insular, comforting silence. He fell into pleasant thought, where colours danced across his world and movement flowed like the occasional beat of birds' wings gliding along the thermals. He sighed and sank into the cushioning malaise.

Night overtook the world. When the veil between worlds thinned to gossamer shimmers, Meran could not decide when or where he was anymore. Beyond loomed shadows, a gathering storm of motion interspersed with sharp, piercing cries like the shrieks of an eagle plunging in attack.

Fear rose with dreaded anticipation. Terror stalked him. It was coming… coming, and he was not prepared. He was never prepared. Slashes of green filled his vision, unbearable heat pounding through his blood like an inferno, sweat breaking out in streams. Before him lay the familiar trail, and beyond it, destruction.

In vain he tried to jerk back, but there was no path of resistance. The power of the vision sucked him in. It hammered him with a plethora of sights and the clarion shrieks of death, no matter his closed eyes and covered ears.

"No, no, no…" Denial played a futile litany. "Not again, not again."

But there was no hope, no help. He would see death replayed until it tore his fragile heart to shreds.

CHAPTER THREE

"Meran! Wake up."

Like rising wind to a fog, the urgent command and rough shake broke through the vision's hold, pulling Meran to the surface.

His eyes flashed open to terrifying darkness. "Who is it?" he cried, as a solid presence loomed over him, churning out of the mists that eddied through the dreamlands. Hideous, grey forms danced at the verge of his mind, stealing his ability to breathe.

"Ellom. It is Ellom." Reassuring fingers squeezed his shoulders.

"El?" Sweat burst in beads over Meran's skin, a residue of fear still gripping him.

"I heard you from the other room. You were crying out in your sleep," Ellom said.

Shivers wracked Meran's body as he struggled with reality, the air ravaging his throat.

"Here, stay with me," Ellom ordered as if he feared Meran would slip back beneath the vision's power. "I'll light the candles."

Pinpoints of yellow-white flared in Meran's peripheral vision, and he tried to take solace in their warm halo.

He found himself safe in his bed, though he did not remember getting there.

"What was it? A vision?" Ellom asked, his familiar face cast in soft spheres of light and shadow. "What did you see?"

Eyes.

Malignant.

Malevolent.

Pools of fiery, roiling lava glaring back at him too immediate to be shaken off.

Meran did not want to remember, but the spectres remained too close to the surface of his memory for comfort. "Ophidian." His voice cracked on the word, a fierce shudder surging through him. Tears slid silently from the corners of his eyes. "Aleia's snake people."

Seership be damned. This magic, this ability to slip into the ethereal realm, was a curse no matter what anyone said. There was madness lurking in the dreamlands. It was a wild, terrifying place where pain and death, anger and fear, guilt and bitterness ruled. He wished now to be done with it all.

Ellom returned quickly, clambering onto the covers, his smaller hands curving about Meran's cheeks. "*Shh* now," he said, words lowered to a croon. "It has passed. You are here with me."

"Only until the next time." And there would be a next time. What had started as a slow and sporadic trickle had burgeoned into a near-nightly onslaught that he had not been able to stop. "I don't know how much more I can stand," he confessed. Emotion tightened his throat and helpless tears scorched his eyes.

Silence descended, his friend's gaze glistening with sympathy.

Meran shrank with shame. To have Ellom witness his weakness, his vulnerability... "It drives me to despair," he whispered.

"You are a seer. Is this not the nature of your gift? To see visions, the path of the future, and to enlighten us thereof?"

Meran sputtered out a bark of laughter verging upon hysteria. "The future? If only."

Ellom frowned. "Pray? What then is shown to you?"

Blood.

Death.

Slashing blades and burning heat preceding the heart-wrenching screams of dying men, hacked, burned, and inundated. A frenzy of destruction that swept all in its wake.

Meran's heart squeezed, his grief a constricting pain that burrowed to his soul. He saw a man with eyes the same striking blue as his own, their familiar, fierce blaze leeching away to nothingness as the blood pooled beneath him. Beorn. Long hair of gold; tall, strong-bodied, passionate, determined, and vibrant with magic, and so like their father.

And despite it all, gone.

He did not want to think of it anymore. "I-I can't say."

"Then don't." Ellom leaned forward, soft but vehement. "I shall never force you to. Let it go." His impassioned tone sliced through Meran like a knife of sanity. Shock reverberated through him.

He felt Ellom's immediacy, felt himself surrounded by the heat of the young man's body, thawing his chill. Ellom's weight kept him from flying apart.

He was not alone. "El?"

Still, he trembled.

"Clear your mind," Ellom instructed. "Breathe. Slow. Slow and deep."

Meran tried to follow, to focus only on the melodic timbre of the man's voice.

"Listen to me." Ellom captured his chin, his gaze drilling into Meran and taking possession of him. "One day you will be ready to bear this mantle. It will not rule you. You will rule it. Meran? Hear me."

"I don't know if I can," Meran admitted. How did Ellom dare to offer him such a hope?

"Well, I do. And you will." Ellom's assurance rumbled deep like an ocean, deeper than Meran's fears. For the first time, Meran saw the man in a new light, and against the backdrop of his terror, he was radiant.

A mindless, desperate desire stirred. "Stay with me," he said. To his relief, the same intention stole across Ellom's features, growing wondrous and blatant as he wiped the flood of tears from Meran's cheeks.

Elation filled Meran as Ellom straddled him, his movements all fluid grace. The warmth and comfort of Ellom's hands held him steady on either side of Meran's head, and he looked into eyes glowing bright with implacable passion. Vital. Imminent. Like a blanket of protection that wrapped about him with its bright possibilities. The immediate threat of the dreamland receded.

"Lie still," Ellom said. Authority resonated in the command. To Meran's surprise, the need to obey thrummed through him.

Again, Meran felt the cushioning aura of Ellom's lustful intensity seething through the air, flooding the ether. Its potent energy hung like a cloud, stifling the echoes of the ophidians' horrifying chorus. With greedy relief, Meran let it envelop him.

As if it had always been Ellom's intent, Meran found his lips crushed beneath a mouth that plundered his. Like a flower to the sun, he opened beneath his friend's direction, all sense sucked from him except the urge to release his pent emotions.

Heat filled Meran's veins, blood rushing to fill his loins. His desperation broke from the chrysalis of his despair into a freeing, feverish imperative to rut. If the hampr had torn open the veil between him and the dreamland, then what Ellom promised more than repaired the damage. With every spike of lust, the terrifying memories diminished, seeking refuge in the mists from whence they had come.

He gasped as Ellom broke their kiss, and Meran tilted his head, offering his neck to the luscious slow pepper of lips as they explored his flesh. Ellom drew mouth and tongue in a searing trail of saliva across his jaw and throat until he fell to nibbling along Meran's collarbone.

Reaching to thread his fingers through Ellom's thick hair to direct his path, the man's low command brought Meran up short. "No. I said, lie still." The order shivered through Meran like a forbidden thrill and all but the thought of what Ellom wanted withered.

In wonder, Meran stared at the familiar, youthful face, now so foreign and mesmerizing. Ellom's gaze pierced him, dominated him, and he found himself in a state of confusion. Never had he been ordered to lie still. And for that order to offer him such peace was confounding.

As the son of a lord marshal, his family were considered patrician; noble, privileged, the authority. His brother had been a beloved commander of men in all things, and if Meran ever wanted to fill those shoes, it was his duty to be in charge in every facet of his life.

Aroused and at a loss, he floundered, wanting only more kisses to divert him.

"I know your way," Ellom said. "But at this moment you are not the son of Durans Durante. You need not be the fount of pleasure that all men drink from. You are Meran, and it is I that will slake your thirst."

Ellom paused as if awaiting a sign that Meran heard and acquiesced.

Meran's breath came deep. He had never even considered it a possibility that he and Ellom could be friends in this manner. Knowing Ellom's tendency to obsess over those with whom he formed attachments, it behoved Meran to step warily.

But unexpected excitement tangled every nerve as relief stole through him, unforeseen and unprecedented. Not alone was the call of the dreamland and all its madness silenced by what they were doing, but a desire, buried so deep he had not known of its existence, surfaced like a volcano. It parted the sea of his curiosity, boiling away any thought of resistance. He was commanded, and he wanted more of it.

"Good." Ellom's eyes flashed with triumph, his knowing smile spreading wide even as he reached to kiss Meran again. It was a jubilant, purposeful kiss that set Meran's heart into a palpitating rhythm of glorious anticipation.

Drawing back a mere hair's breadth, Ellom's exhalation whispered against Meran's lips. "Trust me. Know that I will give you more pleasure than has ever been afforded to you until this very day."

A shudder wracked Meran's body at the bold statement, but if true he would never deny Ellom his attempt. For Meran, rutting was the pinnacle of all pleasure. Better than the taste of good wine, or a succulent feast; better than a cool swim on a searing day.

And if what Ellom offered brought with it the promise of protection from the vision, even for a moment, it was an indulgence he would never concede. With every consideration of capitulation, relief flooded through him.

"You will do only what I tell you," Ellom instructed. "You will lie still. You will not think. You will only feel."

Meran's nod came quickly, his hands vibrating with self-restraint even as Ellom drew back and peeled the covers from him, letting the cool night air kiss over his bare skin.

The thick aura of lust deepened, so impermeable Meran could detect nothing but the reality of his own body, cravings, senses; both thrilling and freeing.

The flattery of Ellom's soft groan of appreciation as he revealed Meran's form to the flickering candlelight had Meran's prick burgeon larger and harder, inexorably drawing his friend's gaze.

"Remember, you are not to move," Ellom repeated. Shucking off his loose britches, he lay across Meran, ensuring they kissed with equal intimacy at both groin and lips.

The slow movement of Ellom's prick caressing his set Meran's balls to tingling. Want overwhelmed him. His entire body tightened in anticipation, ready and willing even though they had barely begun.

The power of his desire swelled, the need to roll his hips and seek that final bit of friction pounded through him.

Surprise and embarrassment flamed in Meran's cheeks as he tried to resist his body's immediate demand.

His only instruction in this was to lie still and do nothing but feel, yet even the thought of maintaining his motionless state already bordered on earth-shattering.

"I want—"

Ellom stopped Meran's words with a finger to his lips and a

soothing, *Shhh*. Still, he seemed pleased at Meran's lack of self-control. "Calm yourself. I'll not have you release until I give my word. Understood?"

Meran shivered. Who was this person? He hardly knew, even as he offered breathless agreement.

With that, Ellom rose from his position and turned his attention to the rest of Meran's body, ignoring the dancing appendage nestled at the base of his pelvis. Everywhere but there was touched and tasted and explored; his neck, shoulders, chest—even his pits suffered a glorious invasion. Ellom breathed him in deep, his fingers tweaking, unrepentant, at Meran's taut nipples.

Meran's body grew hard beneath the benediction of Ellom's caresses. Even more so as the man drew lower and lower, the heat of his soft, clean-shaven cheek reaching out to caress Meran's sensitive, seeking prick.

Again, a selfish imperative to plunge his fingers in Ellom's hair commanded Meran. He held back and shuddered with pleasure at the exertion of his restraint. He did what was required. Ellom would get to where Meran needed him to be in his own good time. And when he did, it would prove the most yearned for and delicious collision.

More so, Meran welcomed the knowledge that he deserved the adulation and praise that breached Ellom's lips. "So good. You are doing so well."

Meran's reward finally came when a firm grip enclosed his straining shaft and lifted it towards Ellom's mouth. Enveloped, Meran cried out as his passions surged to new heights. He trembled and groaned in a fever of need as Ellom swallowed him down.

Drawing back, Ellom lapped over every inch of flesh down to Meran's balls and back again, before repeating. Meran's buttocks clenched as desperation demanded he surge harder and faster into that hot mouth. He vibrated with want and need. "El, please…"

But his pleading only caused Ellom to pull back. Meran could have cursed his friend.

Ellom laughed and chiding, said, "Now, that is hardly nice. I'll have you know my mother and father were well wed at my birth."

Meran flushed, realising he had not just thought the epithet.

"And for that," Ellom continued, "I think I shall turn my attention elsewhere."

Meran whined and repeated, "Bastard!"

Ellom grinned, urging Meran's knees to his chest, exposing him. What came after took his breath, and Meran could think of nothing else, blocked by the rabid tumult of pleasure at the feel of a tongue at his centre. Grounded and present, he keened under the pressure.

Lathered and suckled and invaded, Meran fell to begging shamelessly.

Ellom rose from his work, smirking. "'Tis good that I have not commanded your silence."

Meran gulped. To be silent would be impossible. His precious flesh twitched and shimmied, imploring for the man's return. "Please."

Ellom gave him one last lap, "Do you feel your obedience has been sufficient?"

"Yes! By the gods." He craved the hot, tense pain of intrusion followed by the unimaginable bliss of being filled. He longed for the rough and irrefutable rapture of his arse being tortured by a pounding cock.

"I agree, but first…" Ellom sank a finger deep and stroked until Meran was breathless, that sweet spot within singing louder and more urgently than ever.

"*Please!*"

"You will not release," Ellom said, inserting another finger and stretching him.

Meran groaned. "I won't." But he thought he might. He clenched his teeth as hard as he could, his hands folding into fists that he wished to shove in his mouth, his desire so irrepressible.

"There." Ellom rose, looking about.

"In the anteroom. Top shelf," Meran bit out, hoping Ellom would hurry back with the little bottle of oil he kept there. He could hardly see straight for the sweat dripping into his eyes and the need wracking him, mind and body.

Ellom's grunt resonated with displeasure as his weight lifted from the bed. If this incident dared to repeat itself, Meran concluded, it would be best to keep the little bottle closer to hand. To his relief, Ellom came back, gone for no more than a few seconds.

Ellom resettled himself between Meran's legs, and soon he felt the distinctive texture of cockhead pressing at him, demanding to forge in. More pressure followed, and then fullness shadowed the long slide, filling him with heat.

Mind-bending pleasure chased away Meran's desperation as Ellom began to move, a slow grind ramping into a flesh-slapping pounding. His body vibrated as the man dove and stroked and seared his insides, hitting that all-consuming spot, and Meran reached for his own prick.

"No, you will come on my rod. Nothing else," Ellom said, pushing Meran's hand away.

Meran whimpered, too mindless to protest. He sank into nothing but the maelstrom of feeling, a storm that scoured his being, his gaze fixed on their connection. Ellom's beautiful, curved member disappeared again and again into Meran and swept that glorious place with strokes that built him to a frenzy.

The sight, the sound, the sensations. Meran could not keep his eyes from that tumescent appendage as it punished and rewarded him. His bollocks tightened and his head fell back on a roar as his release ripped free, so acute he did not even flinch as warm spatter hit his cheeks.

The soft sounds of Ellom's own coming followed, and they tumbled down together, clutching each other in a sticky, sweat-soaked mess. Meran closed his eyes and revelled in the power of his climax. It had been almost holy. Even captured beneath Ellom's body, he felt light and free, their combined heat still searing.

He could not move and did not want to. Not even when he felt Ellom shift, his kisses tracing over Meran's cheeks. Those luscious lips opened and Ellom devoured Meran's spill in long sensual licks.

Kisses and licks swept over Meran's jaw, the hollows of his cheeks, his nose, lips. Even his eyelids and brows were not left unattended in the sweetness of Ellom's grooming.

Meran kept his eyes closed, the rhythm of his breathing long and slow. Satisfaction dragged him down beneath the densest of ethereal mantles, the power of release and satiation proving an impenetrable energy.

He savoured the safety, the freedom of that blanket—his and Ellom's—knowing that for once the dreamland's call could not touch him. Only as sleep stole over him did a last thought prickle: after what they had done, what now was to become of their friendship?

CHAPTER FOUR

A week passed in which the effect of Meran's one night of peace faded, allowing his nightly incursions to continue. Memories of Beorn resurfaced alongside the vision. An unanswered ache filled his heart. More than anything, Meran wanted to see his brother again, to feel the strength of the arms that had held him aloft as a child, pretending to be his steed. To relive the fun they'd had.

Beorn could make him laugh until he almost wet himself, tickling him mercilessly... but Meran's memories were overshadowed by the one torturous sight. The life fading from those brilliant blue eyes, endured over and over again.

Several times a night, Meran woke in a cold sweat, the words on his lips, *What are you doing here?* leaking through his despair.

Like an addict, he wanted to seek out Ellom, but his desire was inherently selfish. They had forged a deep relationship over the years, but their friendship had, and would always be, platonic.

At the end of his tether, Meran decided that if a liaison with Ellom had worked to dull the dreamland's pull, how much greater the banishment would be from an assignation between lovers. He quickly scratched out a missive for Ormand and sent it off with one of the messenger boys stationed about the campus. He then set about gathering a feast of wine and meats to begin his seduction.

The knock came not long after and Meran threw the door wide with a smile of expectation only to find another liveried lad in the corridor. The boy thrust a somewhat tattered and dusty message into his hand. Meran fished in the pocket of his breeches and tossed the lad a tarnished coin. His heart thudded a wary tattoo against his ribs as he retreated with the charcoal-smeared paper.

It could only be from Jon. Guilt flared like a bad case of indigestion and he rubbed a sweaty palm across his belly hoping to soothe it. He had still not talked with him, having come up with no answer for the man's plight.

Opening it quickly, he found Jon's graceful, if careless, scrawl. *Meet me on the morrow, ere the supper hour. I have news,* it said. *Gods!* Did this mean the man only just now found out about the lord marshal's decision? Meran had to admit, all had been silent on that front and with his other burdens, his friend's predicament had slipped to the back of his mind. A wave of nausea swallowed him, but taking a deep breath, he gathered his courage. As the cause of its instigation, he had no other answer but to share in the man's disappointment.

He flung open the door to bid the lad to take his answer. "Here, boy," he called, but the youngster was long gone.

A small rumble of amusement tickled Meran's ears as Ormand appeared. "It has been an age since I have been referred to as 'boy'," he said.

Meran took in the strikingly handsome man, forest green eyes, soft fair hair, and a body so beautiful, Meran bet it could rouse the dead. Ormand had not been a skinny lad in quite a while. Meran shook his head and beckoned the man inside. "I just received a note from Jon and was hoping to flag down the messenger. But, never mind. I will tend to it later. Come, come."

A tic of tension flashed across Ormand's features. Meran wondered if it was at the mention of Jon's name, but the man seemed to shrug off any discomfort and accepted Meran's invitation, tailing him inside.

There followed an easy seduction. Good food, idle gossip, laughter, and lots of wine to loosen the inhibitions—not that they had ever had many around each other. As the night grew close and the candles guttered, Ormand followed Meran's lead to the bedroom. Not as a servant of the House of Durante, Meran knew, but because they were the closest of friends, their attraction mutual.

They came together in a feral dance, vibrant with lust. Familiar and hungry. Meran sensed the effusing cloud of passion rising, born of their connection. Hope swelled his heart at the welcome euphoria emerging from their bodies, filling the air with ethereal power. But it lacked that fateful spark.

"Gods damn this for a bad joke," he cried with frustration. "It does not work." The cloud of sexual energy was a poor excuse for the blanket that had grown thick and sheltering with Ellom's commands and Meran's submission.

Much to Ormand's pique and confusion, Meran threw himself from the man's typically satisfying prick, abandoning him in an unsated state.

Meran's vexation turned his own erection flaccid, and he stomped through the darkness of his rooms to curl knees to chin on the daybed, naked and desperate.

Ignoring the soft movement and the warm hand that rested on his back as Ormand settled beside him, Meran felt the damning tears well at the small sign of his friend's concern.

"Do you wish me to leave?" Ormand asked without accusation, the tips of his fingers caressing Meran's back.

"No." His voice cracked. The last thing Meran wished for was to be alone. If he fell asleep, the vision would wreak havoc on his already tumultuous emotions.

"Then what is it? Have I done something to displease you?"

"Gods, no." Meran unfurled, leaning into the man's shoulder, noting Ormand stiffen with surprise at the gesture. Perhaps that was their problem. Despite their friendship, Meran was supposed to be the master, not the other way around. And Ormand—for all that he had fucked Meran into the blankets many a time in their past—he had never tried to dominate him, not as Ellom had done.

In his life, Meran had never succumbed to the authority of a lover until Ellom. They had so wondrously come together; it tore him up inside that he had even considered it. But what if it proved a necessity to mute the dreamlands power? No. It had to be an anomaly, and something he could ill-afford to do again if he were to remain honest with the young man. There had to be another way.

"Will you tell me what ails you? I may be able to help." Ormand tentatively combed his fingers through Meran's hair.

Regret welled upward, a longing ache hollowing Meran's chest at the soothing touch. Why must he always be expected to give comfort rather than to receive it? Yet, he had always felt gratified when his solace had been appreciated. Why would he want to deny that pleasure to someone else?

"Meran?"

Meran hesitated. Could he confess what he had done and its consequence? If he could trust anyone, it was Ormand. They had grown up together, spending years at play or in competition.

As youngsters, they had studied together and experimented with their growing bodies. They had gone hunting, fishing, and Ormand had helped him practice his wrestling technique even though the man's duties kept him from joining in the tourneys at the university. Surely, Meran could tell him this, Ormand would understand.

"I'm named a seer," he began, "but I am nought but a charlatan…" Once started, the tale gushed out of him like a floodgate opening.

"Ah." Ormand took it all in, pondering over Meran's predicament. "I have always rated Ellom, but he is not one to trifle with. You cannot lead him on, not unless you are serious in your attraction."

"I know. I am a selfish cur." His love for Ellom was that of a love for a brother. What they had done together struck him as somewhat unseemly. Yet, there had been something. "That assignation… it did something. It stifled the vision and gave me peace."

"And you thought to try that with me?" Again, there was no accusation. "I'm sore sorry that I could not have been of more use."

Meran pulled back, offering the man a concerned look. "No, it is I that needs your forgiveness." The import of what he had done pressed heavily upon his conscience. For nearly two years, Ormand had demurred from indulging in the ruts that always eventuated at any of Meran's gatherings. Though he drank and conversed and observed, Ormand had taken to pulling back from the physical activity. Meran had thought to remedy the man's obvious self-imposed celibacy.

But he had not asked the cause. Meran already had his suspicions, but when it came to the heart of the matter, he had been as selfish with Ormand's feelings as he had been with Ellom's. "I am the worst of friends. It seems I am ever exploiting those close to me." Taking but never giving. Just like his father.

Ormand rumbled with amusement. "Had you not considered that I might like such exploitation? I am here after all, without coercion."

A welling of gratitude surged through Meran, and the desire to kiss Ormand tugged at him as he sat forward, elbows on knees, a serious cast overtaking his features.

"But here," Ormand interrupted Meran's intentions. "You are not the only one to have ever suffered the perils of seership. Is there not someone at the university that you can turn to?"

"That was my father's intention when insisting I study the mysteries. But none of the masters has one jot of wisdom to offer."

"Hmm. Perhaps you need to begin a search of your own. Is there not many a tome that might offer you such pearls of wisdom to ease your plight? You have access to the most extensive library in all the land of Locurnia. Might you not research an alternative?"

Of course! He had not previously thought of the library. Hope grew warm and enticing in his chest. He would visit on the morrow and attack the oldest and dreariest of scrolls with determination. There had to be writings, if not from past seers themselves, then from those who had lived through their times and had observed their comings and goings.

Meran needed to know how to control his gift, not run from it. After all, what good was a seer who could not navigate the dreamworld? What good a seer who feared to have visions at all?

With a heart filled with gratitude, Meran leaned purposefully towards those lips, so full of wisdom, and kissed Ormand with an intensity of purpose.

And though the connection between them that followed did not create the mantle that drowned out the dreamland's merciless call, it strobed into the stormy night of his soul like a lighthouse revealing the jagged shore of possibilities.

Dust plumed as Meran slammed the book shut, his nose itching with the undeniable urge to sneeze. Latius was not his favourite language and the scratchings were almost faded into insignificance that made the reading impossible.

He glared balefully, first at the worn leather cover—the apparent ravings of Philo Janiusz, a mad prophet, all collected in one huge volume—and then at the burdened shelves, dusty stacks of books, and scrolls that surrounded Meran's secluded spot in the university's vast library.

Meran's disappointment tasted bitter, his fragile hope withering. He had diligently searched the ramblings of former soothsayers, prophets, and seers and now felt he grasped at straws. If they confessed anything at all, it was only the expounding of their visions. Any failings were not committed to parchment.

Meran's neck creaked in protest as he unfurled and stretched out his tightened muscles, his heart sinking even as an ache echoed between his shoulder blades. *Gods damn*, he needed to sleep without the nightmare, without the slashing blades and the slow, screaming deaths of good men made familiar by their nightly haunting.

"Meran?" Jon's well-known voice boomed, echoing through the hallowed halls of the university's library. *Oh, by the gods!* Meran scrambled to his feet. He must be late for their assignation.

Anticipating a snarl from the irate master librarian, he rounded the end of the stacks at pace, knowing that this friend would likely ignore such admonishments.

Across from him loomed dark wooden doors beneath the high arch of the library's entrance. Dwarfed by its majesty, a group of lads milled about receiving a tongue lashing from Master Lucerene, his finger wagging in their direction, his beetled brows forming a thunderous scowl. Jon, in the lead, gave the master a benign smile that seemed to do little other than fuel the master's fervour.

Meran shook his head in amazement, wondering if there was a *Voce* alive that Jon could not tolerate. His other companions looked bored or eager to retreat. Now that Jon had come for him, Meran found himself unwilling to lose their friendship based on the lord marshal's slight. Jon had to know Meran would do anything to make it up to him. He hurried over in time to hear the end of the librarian's tirade.

"That you have had the one successful exhibit" —He tapped Jon on the chest— "does not give you leave to disrespect this atheneum. The masses may not appreciate how you mock them with your salute to debauchery, but I am not so fooled. Off with the lot of you and leave Master Meran to his studies."

This would not do. "Come now, good Lucerene," Meran intervened, his tone deferential, drawing Master Lucerene's sharp pale eyes his way. "After all, my father did sponsor Jon's exhibition. Do you accuse your lord marshal of having poor taste?"

Looking offended, the man straightened to an unimpressive height, barely reaching Meran's shoulder. Meran had grown to tower over most of those in his acquaintance—a trait inherited from his mother's side of the family, though it had passed by the woman herself. Not even Beorn had been of equal stature, although the mere charisma of his presence no doubt made up for any lack.

"Of course not," Lucerene answered. "I imagine him having been quite falsely importuned."

Meran's eyebrows shot up at the bold assumption that his father was gullible enough to back an unknown talent without first having approved of the exhibits.

He turned a warning eye on the older man. The master had all gall to besmirch the Durante name, to criticize his father in Meran's presence. If there was call for censure it would come from a Durante or one above his father's rank. "I consider such presumption an impertinence. Best my father hears nothing of it." Meran grabbed Jon by the arm and led the band of young fellows from the hall, leaving behind the discombobulated master.

"I'm sore sorry you had to suffer that," Meran said as they emerged into the fresh, salt-laden air. "He's always been the pompous sort."

Jon's expression remained unperturbed as they all strode along a cobbled path. The wind off the sea susurrated through the windbreak of greenery and the encircling cream stone walls of the university, playing with their hair and clothes with crisp, cool fingers. "It is an artist's dream to polarise the masses," he said.

"To be divisive, you mean." Meran gave a grim laugh. "Besides, I would have hoped it a dream of yours to turn a few coins."

"Oh, I did not do ill from my exhibition. I'll have you know I sold several works. My talent now graces more than one wall or garden of the most prestigious of the bourgeoisie." Jon smirked. "Someone even paid for the privilege to defile one of the smaller pieces."

"That is despicable," Meran said, offended for him.

"They paid," Jon shrugged it off. "And word circulated. As a result, it seems I have become even more famous. Not their intent, I am sure."

"And your centrepiece?" Meran asked. That sculpture had been a particularly intimate likeness of Ormand, its beauty and majesty causing quite the stir. He hoped Jon could not be so blasé with such a work. The raw-hewn stone from which it was made must have cost a small fortune.

Jon's expression sobered. "That is never for sale, and you know it."

The stunningly crafted piece of marble was now held in storage at Lord Marshal Durans' estate, awaiting Jon's decision on its fate. It seemed even though he had lost his backing, Jon still refused to part with the piece.

Although Meran did not know the details, he knew that there had been some altercation between artist and subject over the sculpture. Ever since its unveiling, Meran's curiosity had pricked, but neither of his friends had cared to enlighten him. Again, Jon was quick to change the subject and Meran lost his chance to enquire.

"Besides, as your dear sire cannot be my patron" —*Ah, he knew.* Pangs of guilt assaulted Meran— "I've had to seek out other options. That is why I have come to you now." Jon's grin returned. "I've had an offer of patronage. Said champion has invited me and my company to his residence for a celebration. I'd hoped that you would join me on this venture as I am more than certain I will need your fine words to impress him."

"Praise the gods!" Relief shattered Meran and he grabbed Jon by the hand, shaking it vigorously, a matching grin of delight spreading his lips. "Congratulations! Of course, I will come. I would not miss it."

Jon's dark grey eyes gleamed and all turned towards the path that would lead to one of the university's many exits, excitement filling every expression.

Only then did Meran's eyes spot a well-known figure, hand raised to wave him down. His heart skipped a beat.

Ellom.

All Meran's suppressed desires flooded over him.

CHAPTER FIVE

The unexpected magnitude of his relief made Meran's face heat. A stuttering storm of excitement arced through him. No matter how selfish he had confessed his feelings were, the beauty of that night with Ellom and the peace that resulted still called loud and insistently to him.

A stab of guilt followed. This was not how it should be. Ellom should have meant more than to be a balm for his shattered, vision-ridden nerves, and yet his sudden yearning overwhelmed him. His memories of Beorn were tainted by the soul-draining repetition of a senseless death he knew only from that one vision. So much so, he could not summon even one good feeling at the remembrance of his older brother.

But with Ellom in his sights, Meran experienced both a desperate hope and unease; nerves squalling and tying up his tongue.

Yet his desire imperilled a friendship that had endured from their youth. He could not allow that to happen. Such weakness diminished him. And he realised, now that he saw the man, he had little faith in his own conviction. It was good he had kept himself from Ellom's way for as long as he had, or he may have done something foolish.

"Ah, there you are." Ellom hurried towards them, blond hair whipping in the breeze and the crisp linen of a long tunic over boots and britches flapping about his calves. A blue cloak billowed at his back and a thick-buckled leather belt sat atop his slim hips.

At any other juncture, Meran would have teased him for his pretentiousness, but now it struck him how mature and striking the garments made Ellom appear, for all his smaller stature. Their last time in company had revealed what a strong-willed and resolute young man his friend was. Having now seen him thus, Meran wondered that he had not realised it sooner.

"Just in time," Ellom said drawing even, his handsome, youthful face flushed. Surges of excitement infused the air about him. "I thought I might have missed you. You were not at your last lecture…"

"I have been ensconced in the library all day," Meran said. "Buried beneath a pile of worthless books."

"Oh." Ellom continued without a beat missed. "Well, no matter. I would have you do somewhat for me."

Meran lifted a curious brow.

"You will come to the Petrel's End," Ellom said, a confident tone infusing his voice and ringing with the very thing that had set Meran's heart to fluttering.

Meran felt a shiver traversing his length, pooling with a passionate hum in his nether regions as he considered where it could lead. Again, heat flooded his face, embarrassed that he could be so affected.

"Ah." This proved even more awkward than first anticipated. If he went with Ellom, he could surely secure another night of peace. But at what price? And he owed Jon. He could not abandon him now. "You wish me to come this minute?"

"No. I have an interview with the board this eve," Ellom said. "They have invited me to dinner along with a mere few other applicants. This might elicit entry to study beneath Master Romaine." Ellom shrugged almost shyly. "I would have you meet me after…"

Jon, gesturing for the others to head out, distracted Meran from his sudden indecision. "Meet us at the back of Little Summit Street," the artist called after their retreating friends and then smiled his greeting at Ellom. "A drink at the Petrel's End, eh?"

Ellom's transparent expression broadcast that his offer had not been meant to include Jon. Meran's careening senses were slapped back into place. This very attempt at exclusivity was a concern. He knew he must do nothing to encourage any misunderstanding between them.

The other night's assignation had not been the invitation Ellom seemed to anticipate, and that was the crux of the matter. Meran was torn between the desire to go with Ellom, knowing what would surely follow, and honouring the obligation he had to Jon. Without Meran's bad behaviour Jon would assuredly not be in his current predicament. He owed Jon his loyalty and support in his pending endeavour, even though an urgent and greedy part of him yearned not only for peace but the rapture of his own sexual submission.

"I'm sore sorry," he addressed Ellom, "But you find me at a time when I have a prior engagement."

"What? With Jon?" Ellom's expression dropped.

"Aye. And as I'm certain you will charm the masters perhaps we could all accompany you on the morrow eve to celebrate?" Meran answered. If he must suffer the dream's invasions this night, then the following eve he could allow himself to do something considerably more foolish with Ellom braced with a bellyful of wine. For a few moments, he might not even regret it.

Ellom's cheeks blazed, dissatisfaction contorting his brow, his throat working as if words crammed his windpipe, trying to explode outward.

"That's a fine establishment," Jon said, filling the impotent silence, and seeming to consider Meran's suggestion as if his inclusion were not blatant provocation. "And a bit beyond my current means."

"It's the Petrel's End," Meran interjected, "not the Gold Falcon. Anyway, I'm sure your financial predicament will not be for long. Not once we've visited Little Summit Street."

Jon nodded. "Indeed, I'm confident my potential benefactor will come through. We need not cross all fingers and toes, at the least."

Ellom's firm features took on a curious cast. "Little Summit? What takes you there?"

"Jon's found a possible sponsor and we are invited to…?" Meran directed a questioning look at Jon. He had not even thought to ask.

"The Villa Bardi," Jon answered. "It seems that its master was impressed with my pieces."

"Pray, what?" Ellom's face paled. Rudely, he tugged Meran aside. "What are you thinking? You cannot go there! Do you know whose estate that is?"

Meran shrugged, stifling the surge of indignation at Ellom's supercilious tone. "I presume a very old and prestigious family." And therefore, he had every reason to be present.

They both knew Jon did not come from wealth. His family were fisherfolk from the South Coast. Jon had found an advocate and gained a scholarship that had allowed Dun's prestigious university to take him. He did not have connections, bar those made with his fellow students and their families. Meran knew it would be best to have someone navigate the inevitable pitfalls of the privileged for him. And who better than the son of a lord marshal? Even should his father consider him *delinquent*. Meran sneered at what Durans Durante would make of such an opportunity.

Ellom's lips pursed as if he tasted something bitter. "It belongs to the Gratians, that's who. Your father would not be best pleased, especially knowing the current patriarch's predilections."

Meran's brows shot high. "Oh?"

"He may have a wife at his estate on the Summer Isles but rumour says that there is more than one kind of flesh that satisfies him," Ellom announced.

Meran barely stopped his eye roll. "And, your point?"

Ellom had almost sounded worried as he relayed that titillating bit of gossip, but there was no need. The tastes and tempers of the exceedingly prosperous were well known in their circles.

It was accepted that celebrations of the type Jon headed to could end with a round of wanton fucking, but Meran had no intention of initiating with anyone. He had learned his lesson with Ormand. While pleasant, such activities were indisputably futile for the type of relief he sought. Fucking was not on his immediate agenda, he told himself. That was why he had pursued an alternative in the first place.

"Do you accuse me of not knowing my own mind, that I don't know how to behave in company?"

"Of course not!" Ellom seemed appalled at the very suggestion.

"Well, that's that," Meran said as if dusting the issue off his hands.

"Meran!" Ellom's voice tightened as Meran made to rejoin Jon. He pulled Meran to a stop by his ear. "That is not the problem. Surely you know of the feud?"

Grimacing, Meran tugged away, shaking his head with bemusement. Gratian was not a name he had heard linked to his father, and he did not need his friend's overreaction.

"I tell you, there is no love lost between the Durantes and the Gratians." Ellom said, following Meran as he returned to Jon. "It is centuries in the running! For your family's sake, engagements are best avoided."

"For pity's sake." Meran huffed with impatience. "After the Serpent war, who longer holds with ancient and petty feuds? Certainly not my father, nor me. You should not, either."

"It's hardly ancient," Ellom rejoindered. "There remains plenty of competition between Lord Durans' fleet and Rune Gratian's to this very day."

Again, Meran shook his head in exasperation. "It is the duty of a merchant to be competitive. You make too much of it. If you are so concerned, I bid you, come with us."

"I cannot afford to miss my interview, or I risk losing the placement I've sought for the last four moons. Besides," he stepped closer, voice lowering to a whisper, "that was not my plan. I would prefer you to meet with me at the Petrel." Innuendo wound through his voice, a meaningful sparkle lighting the grey storm of his eyes.

Meran licked his lips. One part of him wanted to go, desperately, but he knew he could not risk it. There were too many things that plagued him. Things that he must face. Things he had to put to rights.

His father; his magic; the recurring vision; Ellom's misconceptions; and the loss of Jon's patron. If he could help secure these new funds for Jon, that would be one less debt.

For a moment, the ugly face of selfishness reared its head. Would that he could do what he wanted without reference to anyone. How much simpler life would be? If only that were his lot, but the loneliness of such a path pulled him back to himself. Though life came rife with obligation, the fellowship of his friends more than made up for it.

"No," Meran said. "You must understand that I have promised to help Jon. It is a promise I mean to keep."

To Meran's surprise, Ellom did not argue but turned a furious gaze upon Jon. "Do you not understand how much he has already displeased his father? It is inconceivable that you take him to such an abode and subject him to the lord marshal's further wrath!"

The correlation seemed to mean nothing to Jon. "What do you speak of?"

"The withdrawing of his support," Ellom began to explain, it appearing more than obvious that Jon did not know of Meran's part in his ill-fortune. Meran best preferred it kept that way.

"Now, hold just a moment," he intervened, placing himself between the fiery little man and the discombobulated artist. "This once, I think I may be forgiven for putting Jon's welfare first, don't you?" he asked Ellom.

"I do not." Colour blushed beneath Ellom's pale cheeks. "Why would you even insist this when…" The young man's eyes grew round and wide as a thought came to him. His lips pursed with displeasure. "Oh, I see. You think to find peace in the arms of revelry. Well, I think you would be best served to meet me at the Petrel's End. You know what I have already given you, and I would never hold back."

Ah, ye gods! What a pickle Meran now found himself in. An evening of wine and comradery seemed the perfect distraction but Ellom's offer could only play into further disaster.

Meran swallowed and turned his back to Jon to keep his confession private. Taking Ellom's hands in his, he tried to gather his thoughts. How to say this without ruining everything? "I thank you for the offer, but this is not how I must remedy my dilemma. I cannot put my faith in the one incident between us. I need another way forward. A permanent way to be free of it. It is unfair to all concerned if I stoop to using you. Do you understand?"

"Of course," Ellom agreed, but his eyes lit with hope. "But I can still offer you that peace while you seek this other avenue."

"No, no. That is not the way of it." Meran's exasperation grew. There was more than one reason that commanded Meran's loyalty, and if Ellom did not understand this, then so be it. "I go with Jon."

"I cannot countenance this," Ellom shot back. "And your father will know of it."

Meran scowled, anger suffocating any regret he might have felt at the furore. The choice was not Ellom's to make. His words smacked, not of dominion, but assertion; overriding Meran's self-determination. He would have none of it.

"As you like," he concluded, calling the man's bluff. Ellom might think only to make him see sense, but Meran would not be censured. The more he thought on it, the more he determined to go.

Ellom's hard expression collapsed, wounded by Meran's dismissal.

The inevitable pangs of guilt stirred, and Meran gave in to them. The last thing he wanted to do was hurt the man, the incessant voice of self-preservation yammering that he could not afford to eschew all that Ellom could offer him. If Ellom decided to come, there would be hope; if not, Meran was doomed to another turbulent, heart-wrenching sleepless night. He placed a comforting hand on Ellom's shoulder. "Look, go see your committee and then join us. Please." He imbued the last word with the truth of his yearning. "The invitation is open." They were friends, and he hated to see the rift forming between them.

Ellom's expression remained self-righteously obstinate. Meran's heart sank, the possibilities looming large and inevitable.

CHAPTER SIX

"You have surely put a tear in his sails," Jon observed as the small carriage jounced over the cobbles.

"Ellom does not always know what is best," Meran answered, trying to reassure himself that he had not been too dismissive. After all, what they had discovered together about himself did not give Ellom the right to tell him what to do. Still, he had expected Ellom to accede and say he would join them later. It had come as rather a disappointment that he had not.

"He's probably right about your sire, though," Jon said. "If he and Gratian are rivals, he'll not like that you affiliate yourself with such a one, even if it is on my behalf."

"Mayhap," Meran replied noncommittally. His father might not like it, but his current opinion of Meran could not fall much lower than it had already. From the lord marshal's previous actions, his effusive support for Jon had been genuine. It had astonished Meran that his sire would use the high priest's prohibition for leverage against his own son. And now Jon, upon whom his sire had heaped ebullient praise, now suffered possible penury. No, this deal with the Gratian fellow had to succeed. "I think I may risk his wrath for your sake."

Though he looked doubtful, Jon said no more on the matter. They talked of other things as the horse drew them down Dun's wandering streets. Like a giant bird's abandoned nest, the cottages, villas, and apartments lay like strewn pebbles gleaming white in the late afternoon sun.

As the carriage rolled down a steep street heading towards the outer wall of the city and the bluff on which stood the Villa Bardi, they caught glimpses of the Gratian estate. The breadth of adobe tiled roofing spoke to the extravagance of the buildings beneath, surrounded by an expanse of lush rolling greenery. Impressed, Meran had to admit, it rivalled even his father's own holdings.

39

"Have you ever been here before?" Jon asked as they caught up to the gaggle of young men on Little Summit Street hanging about outside a small gate cut into a white stone wall, now blocking their view of the villa beyond.

"You heard Ellom." Meran threw some coin at the driver as he disembarked from the carriage and joined his friend. "We Durantes and Gratians are apparently at loggerheads. Accurate introductions might not be the order of the day. Call me Ormand for the duration, eh?"

For a moment, Jon looked uncomfortable, but he nodded agreement. "I'll let the others know."

A hubbub of noise greeted them as they met up with their friends. Once Jon had handed his invitation to the guard at the gate, they forged through into a thick shrubbery that surrounded a cobbled path. Stonework arches stood before them leading into an inner courtyard, complete with a bubbling fountain and an array of plants whose purpose was nothing more than to look luxurious.

"Beautiful," Jon said, drinking in the scenery, his face alight with enthusiasm.

Meran knew that look. Inspiration for another masterpiece. Probably of some naked person bathing in the pool. Even Meran could appreciate that; the way the light danced over the cobbles and between the hanging vines cast the area with brilliant rays slicing through the rippling shadows. A setting stunning enough, he might even consider offering to be Jon's model.

"You know, an ancestor—my mother's great, great, however many greats, aunt—owned a vineyard," he said. "The lodgings of which were said to be as spectacular."

"Was she the mad one?" Jon asked.

Meran rolled his eyes. "No. Of my mother's family, there were plenty who were, but not she." Linette Tish. That had been her name. She had been cursed with the same magic as Meran, only, somehow, she had found her peace with it. Pangs of jealousy assaulted Meran. *She probably drank herself into a stupor on a nightly basis.* And this night, if nothing else, Meran determined he would do the same.

"Welcome, gentlemen." A voice interrupted his musing. Meran looked up to see an immaculately attired steward emerge from beneath an arch's shade. "Master Gratian awaits you on the terrace."

They were led through the courtyard into the cool interior of a long open hall. Gleaming marble statuary littered their path. Nude figures of both genders, one even displayed the small breasts of a woman, while between their legs hung the recognisable appendage of a man.

"Interesting." Jon smiled as if amused and reassured by the man's encompassing taste.

"It seems our host is not blinkered by convention." Meran smiled with him, glad that Jon's prospects seemed assured.

Low mutters of awe accompanied the group's journey, the magnificence of the villa revealed in the plush décor. A number of open bedchambers and a resplendent triclinium replete with low marble tables and divans upholstered in magenta brocade lined the tiled concourse leading to a dazzling atrium. Many of the walls were hand-painted with repeated intricate patterns.

"This Gratian is certainly not in want of coin," one of the lads said from beyond Jon's other shoulder.

Bennan sidled up to Meran's right. "They say he has an even more spectacular villa on the Summer Isles where he spends most of his time."

Grinning, Jon reached across and batted him on the chest with the back of his hand. "Best keep such observations to yourself or your words may just bring us ill-luck."

At the atrium's end, a large drape opened to let in the light from the lowering sun, hitting the sea at the horizon. It streamed in to halo a figure that stood beneath an open archway to what must be a terrace beyond. The man himself.

"He's quite the handsome fellow," Bennan said, his words low and eyes bright with interest.

Meran took a moment to study Rune Gratian. He agreed. Tall, broad, ramrod straight. The man stood like a warrior, with his strong clean-shaven jaw and a stature both proud and imposing. An impressive figure—no pampered merchant, even adorned in his long robe.

"Hmm," Meran replied. "Both striking and canny. And with a backbone of steel, would be my assessment."

To that, Bennan grinned as if he found the assumption appealing.

What surprised Meran was the man's soft fair locks that were cut to fall in loose waves about his ears. He knew with many of Dun's most successful merchants it was customary to emulate the culture of their trading partners, but the style only served to emphasize the man's regal masculinity.

While his father's position constrained the lord marshal to leave these duties to an agent, it seemed Gratian could afford to be hands on. Replicating the fashion of those with whom he traded was a bold and sagacious statement.

Rune Gratian stepped forward, his gaze sweeping over the group. "Welcome, dear Jon. And friends," he said.

Startling dark honey-coloured eyes settled on Meran. Meran caught his breath, convinced that he had somehow been recognised, but Rune's gaze travelled on, taking in the rest of his companions with equal hawk-like curiosity. The man finished his perusal, his attention falling upon Jon. "It pleases me that you were able to answer my invitation with all haste."

"Ah, your praise is misplaced," Jon replied, taking Master Gratian's offered hand. "I am but a budding artist. Who am I to turn down such graciousness?" Leaning in, he kissed both the man's cheeks in greeting.

Meran snorted under his breath. It looked as if his own fine words were not needed. Jon appeared to have all in hand, unless, of course, this confidence was a consequence of Meran's presence. Time would tell.

Rune gestured. "Come, come," he said in a voice, vibrant with assertion. "Let us enjoy the last moments of this glorious day ere the festivities begin in earnest."

Even as Rune led the way outside, the nuances of the man's authority startled Meran's nerves to life, his obedience as sure and eager as his friends. The lads clustered about, watching the sun go down as a servant began distributing the first of no doubt many rounds of delicious dark wine.

Meran held his cup and let the aroma fill his nostrils. The deep, spicy flavour with just a hint of tartness filled his mouth with the first sip. A fine vintage, and as excellent as any that might grace his father's table. He gulped it down in two drafts and reached for another. If he thought to follow his ancestor's example, he might as well get started.

"I am sad to see that you have not deigned to bring those who modelled for you," Rune said with lazy reprimand. "I had hoped for a chance to meet the inspiration for your centrepiece from the Civilus. It took my breath."

"I apologise for my oversight. But these are close friends, although friend and model have proven one and the same in the case of one of

42

my wrestlers," Jon answered, catching Meran's eye.

"Ah, a wrestler." Rune followed Jon's gaze. He cast Meran a curious look, raising his goblet in salute.

Meran downed his second drink and accepted another as the servant passed by. A fine buzz began to tingle through his blood, and while it was a welcome beginning to inebriation, he decided caution the better part of valour. He had eaten little all day, and at this rate would find himself on his arse even before supper could be served. For that, Jon would not thank him.

"I had heard the university had acquired your services, Jon," Gratian said. "Indeed, I have witnessed said masterpiece upon my last visit to campus." The man paused for a slow smile, his posture shifting to face Meran. "I must admit, Jon does not do you full justice."

Jon barked a sharp laugh. "Such justice is not always possible when one is expected to make a likeness in limestone. If I could, I would have fashioned them all in marble as I did for the piece you favour, but time was a factor as was the university's limited generosity."

"You are too modest." Rune ran an assessing gaze Meran's length, "The form and lines I judged a thing of beauty, but in person, your model is exquisite. You may be forgiven for not capturing his likeness to perfection." Rune's attention pinned Meran full force. "Of the pair, you were the man to his knees, were you not?"

Meran squirmed beneath that stare, wary of the unbidden thought that surfaced. He did not relish being thought of as someone easily driven to their knees, yet this man might do it. The heat of a blush filled his cheeks. Still, he did not wish to appear flustered. "I was."

A twinkle appeared in those eyes that again swept Meran from top to toe as if seeing through him. "It is nought to be ashamed of," Gratian said. "We all find ourselves in said position more oft than not in this life. So now, sculpture aside, who are you? Your look is familiar. Have we met?"

"Ormand, good sir." Meran held out his hand. A firm grasp enveloped it, inherent with strength. Powerful, composed, confident. Meran felt an answering shiver of recognition travelling down his spine, even as he tried to push his eager thoughts aside.

Could this man be as Ellom? Was there a possibility of peace for him this eve in the form of the villa's master? He did not want to hope. Guardedly, Meran offered the man a kiss to each chiselled cheek.

"We have never been formally introduced, that I know of." He pulled his hand free and took a step back. "But as you say, if Master Gratian has been to the campus, I'm sure that we may have crossed paths. I have not only stood as inspiration for Jon's wrestlers, but I enjoy the actual sport. Perhaps you were witness to one such event where my erstwhile employer" —he pointed to Jon— "happened to do me out of a very fine trophy?"

Rune Gratian laughed a deep rumble, a hand of commiseration resting on Meran's shoulder. "That I can scarce believe."

"Well, believe it you must. He has been gloating these last two or so years. But I assure you, he is a man of many talents. You will not regret your investment."

A telling gleam filled Master Gratian's eye, his gaze stroking over Jon at Meran's praise. Disappointment flashed at the look, and Meran began to suspect the merchant held an interest in his friend of a more personal nature. Understandable. Jon was a fine-looking fellow with his lithe, if compact physique, his storm grey eyes, dirty-blond hair, and his carefree expression. But Rune Gratian would be in for a setback. Meran could only hope Jon's preference for all things maiden would not ruin his chances of securing the merchant as a benefactor.

Of course, this was also Rune Gratian's chance at philanthropy. Meran counted him an intelligent man, enough to know he would earn himself prestige in the eyes of many with this offer. As did any who had the wherewithal to support the arts.

"Master," a servant called. "Your other guests have arrived. I have taken the liberty of showing them to the dining hall where a supper has been served."

Meran's heart stuttered at the announcement. There were to be other guests? He cursed silently.

"Thank you, Maico," Rune said, turning from Meran back to Jon and gesturing for the artist to precede him. "Company awaits, my good sirs. I have gathered a number of my associates who are all interested in the arts. They all wish the chance to get to know a man of such promising talent."

By the gods. Meran's heart beat a rapid tattoo. What if there were any amongst them who knew his identity? Prudent as he had thought his deception had been, he could now be revealed for the liar he had just made himself to be. Then, there would only be disappointment and judgement in those honeyed eyes as they looked at him.

Meran swallowed. Perhaps, even anger.

CHAPTER SEVEN

Would jumping over the balustrade be too conspicuous?

Jon grinned, seemingly unaware of what trouble they might be in for. He followed Gratian's lead, the man's hand falling to the small of his back.

Meran trailed reluctantly behind the bevy of lads, all eager for further entertainment. To make an excuse now would be equally as damning.

A band of anxiety caught about Meran's ribs as he scanned the unanticipated guests. Tall, short, muscular, rake thin, handsome, or plain; none were immediately familiar to him. Yet what should have been relief was tainted with the thought that the world was small. Though it appeared Rune Gratian and his father moved in different circles, there was all possibility that some, at least, were likely associated with Dun's Lord Marshal.

Until this point, Meran had taken little interest in the Durante's business ventures, nor was he invited to meetings. Only those who were of particular importance—other lord marshals, magistars and, of course, the Primoris himself—ever graced the halls of his father's own villa. Merchants and business associates met for negotiations at the port office, either with his father or one of his factors. Meran could not know all of them, and by that token, he hoped that none could know him, either. But he would still have to remain vigilant.

Nerves that he could not suppress rode his belly as he followed their host to where his new guests mingled.

The group of men were of similar age and stature to Rune. While appearing younger than Meran's father, they were of the generation to have lived through the Serpent War—a conflict that had taken many a *Voce* and changed the face of Locurnia forever. For that alone, and for their ability to forge ahead in the aftermath of that disaster, he was prepared to admire them.

They milled about in an open alcove off to one side of the atrium. Rune welcomed them all, introducing Jon with a grip on his shoulders. Rune garnered a satisfactory salute of recognition from each guest, and bid them all to share in the feast.

The tables were spread with platters, heaped high with fruit and breads, and fish in various forms of deliciousness; pâtés, bowls of roe, freshly broiled lobster tails drizzled with salted butter and garnished with lemon quarters, and chunks of smoked fish dotted with small tomatoes.

"Sailfish from the deep-sea swells south of Cora," Rune advised, coming up beside Meran and resting a hand on his shoulder. He gestured with the other to the fillets as Meran pondered what he might be hungry for.

"A delicacy, indeed," Meran replied, trying to dredge his memory for anything he knew of the species, so honoured was he by the man's attention. He knew the inhabitants of Cora's Isle were well known for their skill at harvesting the deepest reaches of the chill southern oceans. "I've heard the waters in most parts are too warm for their kind," he offered, cringing at the imbecilic words as they spilled from his mouth. Such an experienced and travelled man must already be aware of this.

Nervously, Meran scooped some of the pink flesh onto a piece of grilled flatbread with a sliver of soft cheese. He bit down, the tastes bursting on his tongue. "You set a fine table, sir," he complimented.

"Call me Rune," the man bade him with a smile.

"Rune," Meran repeated, his ego swelling at the privilege.

"And, I'm sure I am not alone in this," Rune said, indicating to the fully-laden platters. "Come now, fill a trencher with whatever you wish and join me in the atrium so that we may become better acquainted." Rune took nothing but a goblet and carafe of wine and headed for one of the beautifully fashioned benches that surrounded the atrium's central feature. The tiled pool acted as a drain for when the rains blew in off the sea and poured through the open square in the room's roof.

Not wishing to appear eager, Meran sipped at his wine while watching the man's retreat. Rune sat, eyes landing on Meran's as if the man's attention had been inextricably captured. Maybe their host was not so interested in Jon after all.

The rest of Meran's wine followed in one gulp, and as casually as he could, Meran loaded a plate with Rune's bounty. Taking both goblet and food, he settled down beside Rune, his pulse escalating at the possibilities before him. He tried to tamp it down as the older man refilled their cups.

"Now, tell me of yourself," Rune began, taking a slow sip. "What do you study?"

What to say? He might have taken Ormand's name, but he could repeat nothing of his friend's lessons. Deciding it best to stick as close to the truth as possible without giving himself away, he sighed. "The mysteries."

Rune gave another of his rumbling laughs, the sound shimmering down Meran's spine. "Well, that was said with the least enthusiasm I've ever heard. Is your sire a scholar wishing you to follow in his steps?"

Meran scowled. "No, my sire is no scholar. He seems to feel that I have done nought to date but disappoint him. It was with the intention that I learn the origins of *Voce* magic that he set me to my studies, so I might make up for my many and varying sins." Of course, to his sire's logic, it made sense. With knowledge came power, and with seership came prestige. More than anything, it appeared to Meran, his father wanted a seer with the Durante name. Well, Meran could not be that man.

All *Voce* received training at the manifestation of their magic, but few had the ability to slip into the realm of dreams and visions, even if they wanted to. None had done so successfully for at least five hundred years. His great, great —however many greats— aunt being the last he had ever heard of. The rest, well. They had succumbed to the madness of the dreamlands and he too felt its inexorable pull. Soon, very soon it would take him under. He could not let that happen.

"Oh, surely you cannot boast many of those," Gratian responded, his brow raised in question.

"I am not as adept in my lessons as he might wish," Meran mourned as if that equated to a sin. Missing lectures in preference to outdoor activities did not help his cause. Neither did his participation in the wrestling and the field events at the university, nor spending hours in dissipation to numb the edge of despair that nightly hounded him. Meran cleared his throat. "Here, and yourself, sir," he changed the subject quickly, not wanting to dwell on said failings, "you said you visited the campus, may I ask what took you there?"

"You may," Rune teased, but did not insist that Meran rephrase his question. "When I am able, I lecture on behalf of the merchant's guild."

Ye gods! Meran thanked his stars that he had not attempted to further his lie. Ormand studied under that guild in hopes of furthering his prospects. Rune could have already met him!

Meran blinked, shaking the buzz of wine from his head and shovelling food into his mouth while he tried to think clearly. If Rune had met Ormand already, would he not have picked the man as Jon's model for the *Indulgence* sculpture? No, Meran's identity remained safe. He determined it best to stick to the truth as closely as possible before he lost the ability to keep track of his lies.

More food… and he begged, a glass of water…

"And Jon?" Rune asked, as if he did not see Meran's attempt to somewhat sober himself. "How did you become friends? Such diverse studies hardly require your paths to cross often."

"No. It is not usual, but as said, there are more ways than one to fall into company." Here was a safe topic. Meran fell into it. He regaled Rune with tales of Jon and his adventures, both on campus and off.

Meran relaxed, eating, and slowly accepting more wine as and where Rune offered it.

The noise grew, and again Meran felt the influence of the alcohol slip through his veins. Others joined and left their group like a swarm of bees around a hive. The conversation ran down paths of religion and philosophy, of ethics and business, power, and the distribution of wealth. In all, Meran felt himself a match for those of more experience and wisdom, having grown up with such discussions at the dinner table.

"I have never been to the Summer Isles," Meran answered one of the men's enquiries. "But have spent some time at the house of… a-a lord… in Prince Rane's court in Atena as a youngster." At the last minute, he pulled himself back from mentioning the lord's name. Hoping that none of them would ask later, he forged on, speaking in the Velkor's foreign tongue to show how fluent he had become.

"By the gods, you have a talent," the one who had introduced himself as Rollo exclaimed. "I have traded with the people of Velkor for near on five years now and have not progressed past simple greetings."

"Ah, but should you, then what use would your handsome interpreter be?" another fellow asked. "Well, other than to fuck," he added. "A use, rumour has it, you indulge in like rabbits. Your wife must be relieved."

"You always were a bastard," Rollo shot back, but the offence that could have been taken was not. Much to Meran's relief, Rollo laughed. As did his accuser, as if they shared a secret.

Meran cast an eye on their host. His expression was one of amiable tolerance. Meran could only assume all of Rune's acquaintance were aware of whatever this situation entailed. It spoke to the closeness of the group, reminding him of his own bevy of friends.

He tossed a quick glance around the room, finding most of his companions lounging on seats they had dragged in from the triclinium to the further side of the atrium. Swarming about them was a group of courtesans—both male and female—that had arrived without Meran realising. Musicians, too, played softly, a soothing accompaniment to the hum of voices filling the room.

Most of his fellows were still drinking or nibbling at the remainder of the fare, deep in boisterous conversation. No doubt telling each other bawdy stories of forbidden conquests, more from the fertile soil of imagination than reality. Jon was mid-laugh and looking content, but Bennan, upon catching his eye, gestured wildly, his expression rife with displeasure.

Excusing himself—much to his current companion's declarations of disappointment—Meran wove across the room, Bennan meeting him halfway.

"What are you doing?" the young man accused in a hissing whisper.

Startled, Meran pulled back in confusion.

"You hog the host, and even Jon is pushed to the periphery! You know you must do nought to harm his prospects."

"Of course," Meran said defensively.

Ignoring Meran's assurance, Bennan forged on. "Because you know those bastards at the university did not pay for his works, it was barter for everything his scholarship failed to cover. I'm not even sure if his debt is settled."

"What? Surely they could not have forced him to purchase the limestone and then gift his talent, all for nothing. The very nerve!"

"Indeed. So ensure you do not ruin the eve for him. This is *his* celebration and the master and his friends swarm about you like flies to honey."

"I-I.." Meran was at a loss. He had not meant to exclude anyone. He had been enjoying their attention, wine-fuelled goodwill bubbling through him. Rune and his other guests seemed content to stay in his company, and Jon made no move to include himself. "I do not do his cause harm, that I promise." His amity with these men could only further it, he was certain.

With the abundance of liquor available to him, Jon did not seem to care one way or the other. His normal, quiet introspection—eyes noting everything—had devolved through tipsy to near drunken sot. And just then, Jon's arm crept about a pretty courtesan as she joined him on the couch, his grey eyes a storm of lustful meaning. The woman's full painted lips drew wide in a knowing smile, her eyes sparkling beneath her lashes. Soon after, they were embroiled in the most passionate of kisses.

Noting it, Bennan let out a disgusted snort. "Never mind. His course seems set. For the better or worse, only time will tell. Are you coming, or will you continue in company with that bunch of libertines?"

"Paavo, you old rogue," a man called, interrupting Meran's protest of the description. "I see you are late yet again. The festivities are all over bar dregs of ale."

Striding towards the cluster of Rune's guests was an older man. The oldest amongst them yet, he sported stately features, gleaming blue eyes, and a rangy stature. His long fair hair, liberally salted with white, was twisted into a queue at his nape. His skin glowed with oils which failed to hide the crinkles at the corners of his eyes and across his forehead. Yet he looked strong, able, and confident in an elegant robe of white linen beneath a coat of red brocade with gold-embroidered trimmings.

"My friend, ignore Natan." Rune gestured for the man to join them. "I assure there is still food aplenty to go around."

The newcomer stopped mid-grin, catching sight of Meran looking at him. His smile turned almost to a feral leer, and he boldly inserted himself between Meran and the now-retreating Bennan. "My thanks," Paavo said in reply, though his intense blue eyes never left Meran's face. "But I have had a surfeit of food. It is other that I am hungry for." Directing his next words to Meran, he finished, "And are you not a tempting morsel?"

"Ormand," Rune called, Meran barely remembering that he played that role and that the master was directing him. "Bring my lubricious friend over here so that I may offer introductions before he thinks to drag you off."

Meran's belly fluttered, it now obvious the intent of the night was to fulfil every indulgence. What might that mean for him? Could he obtain his relief from the impending night terrors that awaited him in sleep? Quickly, he hastened to obey, gesturing for the man to precede him.

The group shuffled around to allow Paavo a seat. Rune pulled Meran down beside him, opposite the latecomer.

Maico hurried over with a fresh goblet and poured the man a generous portion of wine, though Paavo's burning gaze never left Meran's.

"This is Master Paavo Perico, a man who spends most of his days at his rambling estate on Kings Isle. We are to count ourselves privileged to have his company. Paavo, this is Ormand, a *scholar.*"

Pertinent emphasis was placed on the last word, so much so, Meran wondered if the new master had mistaken him for one of the courtesans. Perhaps he should be offended, but the thought of a dalliance with such a man was not abhorrent. Not with the amount of wine he had drunk and the vibe of flattery thrumming through the air.

"Ormand is also proficient in the tongue of Velkory; to rival even your own mastery," Rune finished.

"Is that so?" The intensity of Paavo's interest escalated.

Meran stifled a laugh, wondering if the man would be titillated by a whore screaming their pleasure in Velkory. He could imagine those sharp eyes growing wild with lust. Still, he cleared his throat, and greeted Paavo Perico with all the formality inherent in the culture of Velkory, letting the foreign words flow easily. Paavo's smile stretched wider in delight.

There followed a discourse in the language of the Summer Isles. Paavo Perico, it seemed, while holding no particular title, was a man of great wealth and influence. Not so much with the governance of Locurnia, but with the merchant's guild of Atena, the city from whence he had moments before arrived on one of his most prestigious merchant vessels.

"Come now, Perico," Natan interrupted. "Enough of this twittering. You monopolize the lad. Though he makes for a fascinating view, let us all enjoy the conversation."

Meran felt his privilege, his confidence swelling. He relished finding himself the centre of their attention. He was wanted by all of them, and without him even having to do more than converse, no seduction required. Meran preened.

"Then, I would say, it is time we moved on to more lubricious matters," Paavo said. "At my feet, boy," he finished to Meran.

The master reached over and wrapped a hand about Meran's head, tumbling him to his knees, his face almost landing in the man's crotch. A surprised yelp escaped from Meran.

"Paavo!" Rune's voice vibrated with a low warning. "The difference between aggression and mastery is vast." Gratian's attention focused upon Meran, the perfume of lust beginning to fill the air like sparks of lightning. "Lad, come here." He pointed to the floor between his own spread knees.

Meran felt the potent mists begin to swirl at his desire to obey, instant heat rolling through his blood at the surety of those words. Possibilities stirred in his nether region as he caught sight of the substantial bulge distorting the fabric laying over Rune's lap.

At that moment, nothing else existed but Rune's burning gaze. Meran shuffled forward, not bothering to get to his feet, his posture brimming with supplication. A firm hand encircled the back of his neck and pulled him close. Meran's nose filled with the spicy, enticing scent of lust's promise.

The aura about him thickened.

This was the right mix, Meran knew it. Rune would wield that command that promised Meran freedom. The man could offer more than the sating of flesh. He could offer the power of his dominion and command Meran's submission in reciprocation.

There would be nothing Meran could ever teach such a man; no obligation for him to even try. He could relinquish every burden, every thought of inadequacy, of trying and failing to meet his obligations as a son of Lord Marshal Durans. And, most importantly, he could let go the despair at his inability to control the wild paths that drew him into the land of visions. He just had to hand himself over.

"Beautiful boy, you will bend for me." Said quietly, Rune's words were no less assertive. The promise, the urgency took a firm hold of him and Meran nodded without question.

Rune's lips pressed hard to his, forcing his mouth open and stealing his breath.

"Come now, Rune, it is not like you to be greedy," Paavo said. "You have already had his company to yourself for the entirety of the evening."

Rune drew back, consuming Meran with his golden gaze. "Ah, but this one is special. Aren't you, my dear scholar?"

Meran did not know how to answer.

The mesmerising stare never left Meran. "What say you?" Rune asked, his attention rife with curiosity and his tone encouraging, perhaps hoping to persuade Meran to take his part. "Dare I deign to share you with these salivating wolves?"

Meran hesitated long enough to take in the group of men clustered about him. Wealthy, privileged men in their prime. A combination of elegance and arrogance and a radiance of health reminiscent of youth, though they exceeded his own age by at least five decades.

At twenty-and-five, to them he was a youngster, and yet few looked much older than he did. They were strong and more than appealing. Neither the thought nor the number overwhelmed him. Orgies were common practice amongst the scholars of Dun. Meran had partaken in many, a glorious mass of writhing and rutting bodies slipping over and into each other in every possible capacity—but never had he been the centre of attention.

And now, the coruscation of their rising passions formed a gossamer mesh of power, enclosing him. The warmth of wine bubbled through both his blood and his head, the fiery intensity of his curiosity urging him to take their offer.

But could he trust them?

He fixed his eyes on his host. He could not deny he wanted what he saw promised there. The man's command, Meran's obedience, spiralling passions, tumultuous release, wonder, praise, and all a catalyst in the forming of the thickest and most impenetrable of mystical blankets. He determined that he could trust Rune Gratian.

"Command me," he said to Rune, his voice edged with certitude, "and I will not disobey."

"Ah, that is a yes?" Gratian radiated triumph amidst a depth of anticipation that set Meran's stomach and thighs aquiver. "I will claim host privilege. What say you?" Rune turned to his fellows. "If you abide by my authority, I think you may join Ormand and me in the second triclinium."

Rune received nods of agreement and in turn Meran received impatient and fiery stares of hunger that filled his chest with the warmth of pride.

"Come." Gratian gestured. "The night moves on, and it is time to take this celebration to the next level."

CHAPTER EIGHT

Upon reaching the semi-privacy of the smaller of Rune's two dining rooms, the master stepped up to Meran, his closeness bringing the thrum of his sexual energy within reach. What was it, this power, this energy that vibrated through Meran's mind like the resonance of a beating drum? It seeped into his pores, clinging to him, the very air stolen from his lungs as Rune leaned in to kiss him with a purr of satisfaction. He felt the possession, the demand in the man's stance, in the grip of his hands curving about Meran's shoulders. He established his dominance in a way that sang through Meran's body, a song of recognition.

Rune luxuriated in the dispensing of kiss after kiss, mouth overwhelming mouth. A hot, wet, greedy claiming, so strong, Meran forgot the presence of the other four who had followed them into the room. Until that was, Rune pulled back, and under the man's direction, Meran's garments fell to their rapacious hands.

Stripped bare, Meran could see the appreciation on their faces, feel the lust building within them. They wanted him, wanted to sate themselves with his body, to indulge every whim, every avaricious fancy. If not for Rune, he would have directed them himself. Would have taken what he sought from their hands, but Rune's aura bloomed with the fullness of desire—not alone to sate both their passions, but to rule them. Like fog rolling in from the sea, it submerged Meran, sparking in his mind and on his skin. His very capitulation took that rolling mantle and bound it to him.

Relief flooded him. No hint of the dreamlands could penetrate, no guilty accusations or the incapacitating feelings of worthlessness and despondency could disperse its satisfying power. Meran fell under Gratian's spell and under the influence of his voice, as did all others who the man bent to his will.

Meran was not so craven, however, that he could not sense the power play between his host and the guest, Paavo Perico. But the older man could never win such a fight, even though Meran fell into his arms and his kisses. Because Meran did it at Rune's request, the desire to please and to be praised by him rising like a ravenous need. Gratian was as Ellom, and Meran's reward would be a night of peace. His gratitude rose, demanding he do anything for the man who could bring him such relief.

"I will not bind your hands," Rune said. "You will bind them with your will." And Meran did. Though he craved to reach out and touch, to run fingers through Gratian's hair and pull him close, he restrained himself. To be denied and to resist was to conquer self, and Meran gloried in his victory and Gratian's fulsome and passionate praise.

Stepping back, Meran's host lowered himself to a chaise, but still he controlled all in the room with his eyes and his commands. Only Paavo Perico pushed the boundaries of the host's privilege, ignoring the tenor of Rune's stipulations while doing nothing to incite reprimand.

Meran's chest rose and fell in panting gasps as the men slid fingers and palms in devastating caresses along limb and groin. They mapped his thigh muscles, surveyed the contours of his taut stomach and stroked the breadth of his chest, tweaking his tanned, budded nipples. They explored the deep dimples at the upper reach of his buttocks and curved their hands around the firm mounds of his arse.

Meran found himself carried away by desire. The stimulation of touch had him trembling with longing, the evidence of his enjoyment rising high and proud.

"Not yet," Rune reprimanded, as eager fingers crept to encircle Meran's erection. Regretfully, they slipped away again, their owner's eyes flashing a hint of contrition Rune's way. Laughing, Gratian relented, somewhat. "You may taste anywhere but there."

And taste Meran they did, with all earnestness. Tongues glided over every part of him while still abiding by Rune's restrictions.

Meran shot Rune a pleading gaze, an entreaty he hoped his host would not ignore. To his relief, Gratian rose to his feet, his advance forcing the others from his way. The wonder and warmth of the man's hand brushed down Meran's shaft. Power poured from him, swelling the shroud about Meran's mind, the blanket of protection now full and impervious. At last, Meran could sink into the pleasure these men offered him, safe in the knowledge the dreamland's call could not penetrate his sleep this night. He was free to indulge, and he would to the fullest.

He ached when Rune said, "This will get what I want only when I want it. You understand?"

Meran's whole body shivered with desire, his prick jerking beneath the man's touch. The purity of his feeling overwhelmed him, his throat working, but no words could break free. But he must. Meran felt compelled to give an answer, even though his greatest yearning was for a firmer and fuller touch to incite his tension further.

"I do, sir," he said, his voice a breathy exhalation.

A satisfied kiss followed, Rune's hand grasping about the back of his neck in a possessive hold. Gratian kissed like a beast, all tongue and saliva—invading—and Meran revelled in it, almost bereft when the man pulled away. He followed as if to beg for Rune's return.

"Present yourself," Rune said, halting him. A surge of anticipation thudded through Meran's body. "Over the chaise."

Wonder and expectation escalated, mingling with uncertainty. What now would they do to him? He bent over the back of the long reclining chair and reached back to spread himself, basking in the words and low sounds of appreciation coming from the gathering. Whatever they intended; Rune chose it.

"Such a luscious sight," someone's whisper teased Meran's hearing. He thought, Paavo, but it was not the older merchant's praise that Meran yearned for.

"That it is," came Rune's reply, thick with desire. "Give it pleasure. I would have him writhe on your tongue."

Meran found himself pushed hard against the backboard, his prick pinned between his body and the furniture as his hands were pushed aside and replaced by a firm grasp to each cheek. Heat brushed between them. An unyielding and demanding warmth captured his sensitive flesh. He sensed greedy gazes roving over him and felt the presence of the others surrounding him, as he moaned under the administration of lips and tongue.

He lost himself, groaning in mindless pleasure. Whoever it was who attended to his arse with such passionate prodding and enthusiastic libation soon had saliva slithering between his cheeks and dripping from his balls. It sent his senses reeling and his desire clambering to new heights.

A cock came into view, and with Rune's order ringing in his ears, Meran took it in his mouth. He loved the feel, the texture and flavours of congress in all its forms, and he bathed the phallus with his attention because he hungered for it. Enthusiastically, he swallowed the sweet cum that soon shot over his tongue from the man's stubby prick.

He loved the gratification the use of his body gave, someone in the throes of passion having once declared his was a body to be used and used well. And he harboured no illusions that these men used him, but he knew he used them in return. The lightness of his spirit at the night's prospect was almost euphoric.

All would garner what they would. They, satiation—him too—but, thanks to Rune, he had also secured his relief, peace, distraction, exhaustion… acclamation.

Someone new replaced the now replete man in front of his face, naked thighs covered in a dusting of pale hair. Strong, defined, muscled. Meran began to lift his eyes, even as a finger rested beneath his chin and tilted his head back. Meran's gaze rolled over the ropy, muscular landscape, fine hair scattered and curled almost everywhere. The expanse of skin, tanned like fresh leather, sported a scar nestled beside a wide, dark nipple. He found himself staring into the honey-coloured eyes of the man himself.

Rune's smile combined gentleness with unyielding determination. "Take me," he ordered.

Meran licked his lips in anticipation as he glanced over the turgid offering. He opened his mouth, Rune sliding between his lips with a burst of flavour that spoke of heat and tenderness, dominion and connection. Meran's mouth filled with saliva.

With firm strokes, Rune eased fingers through his hair, even as Meran himself surged downward. Rune shuddered as Meran swallowed him, the man's sigh soft and delirious. "Ah, beautiful, my boy, so beautiful."

"Stretch him," Rune ordered his companions even as he pulled back to allow Meran a gasping breath. "I want his moans to course my entire length."

The administration to Meran's nethers stopped after one last searing kiss that sucked what felt like his entire pucker between tight lips. He groaned, whimpering at its sudden loss, but that luscious titillation was soon replaced with the warm, hard probing of one, then two, fingers.

Moans rattled through him at the very thought that fingers from more than one man thrust and stroked and widened him and set his sensitive nerves to singing.

"More. I want to see him gaping," Rune said on a breathless note. Pride swelled within Meran that he had been able to so arouse the man.

"My cock would do a superior job." The voice of Paavo rose from behind Meran. With his mouth stuffed full, Meran could only groan his agreement. He yearned for that hard fuck.

"You'd like that, young scholar?" Rune said between pants, ignoring his guest, his hips working uninterrupted. "But, I think... not yet."

Disappointment blossomed, but Meran would not demand nor think, only trust. He would allow himself to fall to their touch and do nothing but take it.

Already, his loins pulsed with an insistent ache, dying for caresses. He craved the irreplaceable pressure of a hand or the burning friction of another's flesh pressing against his, or the solicitude of a beguiling mouth. His body tingled from his scalp—Rune's fingers latched in his hair—to the heaviness in his balls. Tremors of anticipation quaked in his thighs and the back of his legs, and his toes dug into the rug to keep his place.

The feverish assault on Meran's mouth paused, and catching his breath, Rune addressed Paavo. "Of course you would think your cock superior, friend, but I would have you step back. You—"

Meran had no idea which one of the men about him Rune had ordered.

"—get the bowl of oil from the table. You and the others will prepare him for our impatient Paavo here."

Sensation blurred, the conquest of his mouth by Rune resuming even as slick fingers invaded and stroked over and over between his buttocks. A roaring monster of need and desire awoke within Meran. And not just within him—the taste of arousal and excitement flooded his tongue, yet it was not the ultimate culmination from Rune that he longed for.

"Not yet," Rune said, his breath heavy. To Meran's dismay, a hand reached down between his mouth and its master to squeeze a halt to the turmoil of his host's own enthusiasm. Rune pulled back to allow another to take his place, and Meran experienced a whole new plethora of tastes, textures and scents.

Those fingers that had so firmly held his head in place fell to his buttocks, gripping tight and spreading. Meran could almost feel the intensity of those eyes as they took in the sight of his readiness.

"Such a greedy hole," Rune said, the pad of one finger rolling through the slick oil coating Meran's crevice and joining the others within. Meran growled needy rumbles, groaning around the protrusion filling his mouth and writhing on the multiple intrusions in his arse. It was all as Rune wanted. "I think our young scholar is ready for a good pounding. Paavo?"

The feel of naked flesh brushed up against the back of Meran's legs, a turgid rod slamming in to replace disappearing fingers. Paavo cried out in delight, his pleasure echoing over Meran's head as brutal hands grasped his shoulders, then began a ruthless hammering.

Paavo shouted with glee. "Such a mouth-watering sight, is it not?"

Pain burned and passion coiled. Meran found himself dragged back into a demanding set of arms whereupon one of his legs was lifted from the floor to allow another access to his jouncing bollocks. His balls were enveloped in the cavern of a hot, wet mouth, even while another man's descended on his straining erection, taking it in deep.

Suckled, lathered, and pummelled into a quivering mess of submission and blinding need, Meran groaned. Gasping and pleading, he dissolved into a mass of twitching nerves and a roiling fire of passions that burned brighter and brighter.

It was too much, too immediate and overwhelming, and he sank into a whirling pool of jangling desires. Rising pleasure exploded behind his eyes, need and desperation rushing for expression and he hurtled towards oblivion.

He surfaced to find himself seated upon familiar furred thighs, tears coursing his cheeks. The arms about him were no longer Paavo's, but Rune's. As were the kisses that sizzled along the cords of his neck and the tongue that lapped up his salty tears.

The heat of the man's torso burned into Meran's back, Rune's hands falling from caressing and twisting Meran's nipples to sliding beneath his legs and rolling them upward. Exposed, Meran arched, Rune's command issuing with urgency, "Paavo, guide me into him."

A beauteous invasion slipped deep, Meran's body quivering and shaking as he felt Rune's thickness overwhelm him. He shivered and groaned, Rune's solid prick gliding over the spot within, sensation blasting through Meran's core.

He slumped back in a quivering mess. His body consumed the rigid shaft greedily, and he was consumed in turn with the rise of urgency and bliss.

Tugging him down, Rune slid lower on the chaise, and rolling his hips, he exacted slow, building thrusts. "Hold him," he said. Paavo's fingers encircled Meran's legs, keeping them aloft and open. Meran's glassy gaze settled on the older man now crouched between both their legs and leaning in to sample their connection. He groaned at the glory of the sight as much as the pull and tug of Paavo's tongue where Meran and Rune joined.

It proved too decadent, too beautiful, too much to hold inside. Meran threw his head back, his vision floating towards the ceiling, past a distant shadowed figure in the doorway. A pang of dismay reached for him at the sight of stunned grey eyes and a familiar visage. But like dew on a sunny day, it evaporated in the face of his euphoria. He floated away, rising beyond the restriction of his body.

He was nothing but a receptor for passion. He could not see, only feel, just as he needed to. The torturous, tumultuous tunnelling claimed possession of him.

It could not be stopped. He could not think beyond the pounding of his flesh, even when he was lifted and thrown to his back, Rune on him in a frenzy. The intensity saturated every fibre of his being. Honey eyes imbibed every nuance of his shifting facial expression, every telling grimace and every groan that passed his lips. Open and accepting and needy, Meran became nothing but a heaving, jerking receptacle of desire.

Higher and higher he rose on a wave of pure exigence, every particle of his body thrumming with the necessity to explode. And he did. Streams of white droplets shot forth between him and the body possessing his. It spattered them both, even as Meran felt pounded and finally filled with a vibrant, powerful warmth.

And yet, hidden beneath the incomprehensible imperative of euphoria, apprehension needled him. Down and down with him, it went. Was what he had done truly enough to blunt the dreamland's insistence?

Sleep came. And with it, flawless, consuming darkness. Despite the low thrum of concern, Meran sank into it as a babe into the loving arms of its mother and suckled the sweet teat of oblivion. It was called hope.

CHAPTER NINE

Meran's heart pounded, the familiar sulphuric stench invading his sleep. *No! Not now.* Surely it had not been long enough. But, inexorably, the billowing mists swirled through the blackness, surging towards him, covering and clinging.

The blanket of protection was gone; dissipated into the ether with time. And on its tail, ghosts floated. Ethereal voices of pain and panic.

Meran tried to draw away, to force his eyes open and awaken before the vision rolled over him like a shattering wave.

Encased in his sheets, his body lay paralysed, alone, drawn into the horrifying vortex surrounding him. He was powerless to stop it.

Hopelessness followed, despair biting at his heels. He did not want to live through it again. It was passed. Done. Immutable. He could change nothing. All this vision created was a damning sense of futility and heartache that he desperately desired to ignore.

Wet heat pressed down, the immensity of shadows crashing over him. Aleia's jungle. Tall trees spiralling into the far-distant sky. Mists lying heavily on the treetops and vegetation growing so thick his simulacrum, though little more substantial than a puff of smoke, could barely penetrate it.

Anger surged through him. One night was all he asked. One night of freedom. The scream of rage boiled to the back of his throat. He had endured the sight of his brother's death more times than he could count. A brother who, as a child, he had worshipped; as a young man, he had hated for leaving him to his mortifying fate.

Meran's cry spiralled skyward, phantom lungs burning. But the vision churned along, heedless of his distress. *Not again! Not. Again.*

Still, he saw the band of men march towards their doom. In their lead, the tall, familiar figure of Beorn. Soon, they would breach the jungle verge and break out onto the deceptive ground, latticed with streams of boiling mud that encircled the isle that later became known as Ustra.

"Beorn, Beorn! Turn-about," Meran ordered, but they followed their fated course. Wary though they were, their eyes peeled for their enemies, they reached the dreaded shore of the fire river, a churning, roiling flow of white-yellow lava that enclosed the land beyond Beorn's reach. Beorn stared in wonder at the glorious promise of the isle behind a dome of encapsulating power. A tall, central peak rose to the clear blue sky, the land verdant and alive—heaven in the midst of hell.

Meran drank in the sight of his brother greedily. A bold and brave man that none but he had seen in a score of years. These seconds were dreaded but precious. Beorn; hale; vibrant and vital. Almost exactly as Meran remembered.

But there were differences. His brother's cast was now grim, his posture taut with suspicion. Sweat and mud spattered Beorn's gear, and he hefted a sword in hand and at the ready...

The creatures rose and Meran's heart ached for the futility of the loss that would come.

Meran closed his eyes, shrinking back from the inevitable. He could not watch, but still the vision washed over him.

The snake people surged from hiding, the boiling mud heaving with their bodies as if it spewed the living dead from its depths. Aleia's creatures did not burn in its heat, nor did they drown. Beorn's men stood no chance. Pulled down, their shrill screams already echoed through Meran and pierced his heart.

Those who were not taken, ran; their desperate retreat futile. Back to the jungle they fled, only to be met by a horde descending from the trees. Meran saw again the glints of light on metal as the men of Locurnia slashed back at the masses. Blood sprayed like rain and screams echoed as death came for them all.

Meran curled in on himself and screamed with both desperation and rage at the injustice. It had to stop. He could not watch Beorn's slaughter again. "I will not," he shouted, his head thrown back in defiance.

Something brushed his face. Something ethereal. Soft...

Meran froze, the sound of his heart echoing in his ears. "Wha—"

Flurries of snow filled the sky, falling gently into the jungle and dotting the vegetation. They floated over him in a slow, graceful dance, like refreshing kisses; cool, calm, tranquil. The cries of battle fell away, and in awe, Meran reached out a hand to capture the descending flakes.

Touching his shade, they melted as they would if touching his real hand.

Impossible.

He looked skyward, the soft flecks tickling across his face. Light. Persistent. Again and again the snow settled, trickled down his cheeks and tickled his nose and lips. *By all that is holy!*

"Sofie, stop that!" Patrice's familiar voice pierced through him.

Blessed reality called from beyond the veil of cloud. Meran's hands glided skyward, almost expecting to feel Patrice's answering grasp there to rescue him. Such relief flooded him! Here hovered his salvation.

"I only wanted to awaken him." Sofie's childish voice floated on a whine.

"Tickling his face with that feather is not the way of it."

No, no, no, Meran wanted to protest. It had worked a miracle, even if he had no idea how.

"When he's with the ghosts, you must be gentle," Sofie said, her voice a quiet reproach.

"Pray, what? How do you—Oh, never mind. Please, Sofie, move aside."

There ensued more grumbles, like rumbles of thunder rolling through the cloud. The earth shook, vibrating straight through Meran's shoulders.

"Meran?" Patrice's impatience rocked him as aggressively as she shook him. "Wake up, for pity's sake! 'Tis almost the midst of the afternoon, you lazy sot."

"You're supposed to call him, sleepyhead, not sot." Sofie protested. "You always call me sleepyhead. I like it."

"I'll call him more than that if he does not rouse himself before the next grain of sand falls."

Meran groaned, even though elation rippled through him. *He was free…* and something had happened, something that promised change. His hope grew tremulous until he realised he had no idea what had just occurred, nor how he could repeat it.

Gods damn!

"I am awake, for the gods' sake," he said on a snarl of dissatisfaction.

Meran opened one bleary eye. For a moment, scattered memories of the previous night flooded him—at least the little that was still clear enough. By night's end it had all become a blur of more wine, more rutting, overstimulation, inebriation, and eventual exhaustion. Still, his body ached in a most satisfactory fashion. And yet, embarrassment flooded his cheeks. "Sofie?"

The eyes that sparkled at him, he realised, were the fiery dark amber of the youngest Durante. Meran swept a hasty gaze about his surrounds. He breathed a sigh of relief, comforted to find himself in his own bed, in his chamber in his rooms at the university's student halls. The afternoon still shuttered out by the thick drape across the small window.

How he had got there, he did not remember. One of his friends no doubt, sober enough to know when they had all outstayed their welcome. Still, his head ached, his throat thick with thirst.

"You're all dirty," his little sister declared. "And smelly, and you've got no clothes on." The little girl leaned on the side of the bed and bounced on the balls of her small feet. "Everyone wears nightclothes to bed. Silly, silly Merry."

"Oh for goodness' sake." Patrice drew his attention, her voice crisp with exasperation.

"By the gods' hairy ball sac, don't start," he groaned, not wishing to hear the tirade of reproach he felt coming. "It was but a few drinks with the lads." *Oh, but it had been so much more.* It may not have proven the unmitigated success he had hoped for, but the desire to revisit it was insistent. The man, the memories, the power of Rune Gratian's command, every flash sent tingles of anticipation through Meran, just thinking of all he had done. His behaviour should have been mortifying, but he could not convince himself to ignore the tantalising pull of want.

"*Shh.* Those are words Sofie does not need to hear."

Patrice's scolding brought him back to himself. With a dull, unwanted thud, he felt a moment's contrition.

"And from your looks," she continued, "it was much more than a few—and with more than *the lads*, or so I hear. Be that all it were, I would not be here." Patrice filled a goblet from a small jug on a tray by his bed and held it out to him. Though it proved warm, he took it and gulped it down.

"Da's right angry," Sofie said. "His face got all red like a 'mato." Her eyes glowed as if the notion tickled her fancy.

Ellom's words came back, sharp and damning. *There remains plenty of competition between Lord Durans' fleet and Rune Gratian's to this very day.* But perhaps this visit had nothing to do with Master Gratian. How could his father even know? The grounds of Villa Bardi were surrounded by high stone walls, and the internal ones were tiled with marble. The magic of *Voce* farsight could never have penetrated the party's privacy.

"Pray, what?"

Taking the mug again, Patrice answered, "Though it may not be to your liking, father is well aware of your destination last night *and* the men with whom you deigned to carouse. To say he is unhappy is to state more than the obvious."

"How?" Meran's heart dropped. *How could the man know? Was one of Gratian's friends acquainted with the lord marshal after all?*

"Ellom was concerned for you," Patrice replied.

Ellom had gone to his father? Even though his friend had threatened it, Meran had never expected Ellom to follow through. He felt the stab of betrayal, followed by a sharp snarl of annoyance. Why could he not have kept from his business?

"You have been summoned. Father commands you attend him within a turn of the dial. I caution you to listen—"

"I always listen."

"Yes. And then do what you will anyway, taking little thought for how your actions reflect upon our sire. He is the lord marshal of this burg, for the pity's sake, Meran! Why do you continue to pour shame all over his head?"

"By the gods!" Meran couldn't contain his frustration at his sire's apparent hypocrisy. "I tell you, that man is a mystery to me that I will never know. He is happy to fund an exhibition containing lewd content including a nude likeness of one of his servants and yet thinks to hound me about my virtue? We do not live in the benighted age of the cross-over."

"Well, I would not make that your argument," she warned. "Not if you wish to see the light of day again. This is serious. You cannot just go fu—" Patrice threw Sofie a pointed look. "—*consorting* with any men you want. You must think of the consequences for our clan."

"What consequences? It's not as if I'll ever get any with child." Frustration and anger twisted his lips. Why should he be denied his pleasures just because they differed from his father's?

"But that is the very point. You will have to achieve that end someday, and this wild behaviour stands to ruin your chances of making a suitable match."

"Why?" Since the ending of the war and the demise of the Voltan

Dynasty, Ivo Dee had set himself up as Primoris and had transformed the political landscape of Locurnia. There were no more dynastic positions. The next Lord Marshal of Dun, once his father had either died or acceded his position, would be sponsored by the people and confirmed by the then Head of State. It was not like Durans Durante needed an heir.

"You're being foolish," Patrice said after he had voiced his opinion on the matter. She rose from her place and walked to the antechamber, no doubt to get him a set of clothes in which to attend the pending interview with his father. "There are the properties, the fleet, the coin, and the investments, the retainers, and servants to consider. There has to be a Durante heir."

"Then I give you leave to produce him. You are far better suited to it. At least you have a womb." Meran grabbed his robe and, sliding it about himself, rolled from the bed. Ignoring the jolting pain that assaulted his head, he made to follow. "Surely you cannot expect me to marry?"

"Many of your persuasion have done so before and done so successfully, even if it went against their want."

"I can't. I-I just… I don't…" Meran's stomach dropped. He could think of nothing worse. He might as well be expected to marry a bear for all the attraction women held for him. "There is none that can satisfy me. And I don't see why he doesn't allow you to fill such a role. You want to marry, at the least."

Patrice emerged carrying a soft cream tunic, dark green buttoned breeches and an embroidered cloak, a sour look on her face. "Do I?" Her tone dripped with scorn.

"Well, you'd have to stop fraternizing with the servants first," Meran replied with equal bitterness. He knew well, Patrice's current paramour—a man for which he himself had carried a flame for many a year, unrequited yearning being the only outcome.

"Don't you say another word." She stopped him with a warning stare. They stood glaring at each other until he felt the heat of shame flood his face. There had been some altercation years back, some contract offered by a less than worthy suitor and at her continued refusal, damning and hateful rumours had been spread. She had never had a fitting offer since and, for all he knew, was the happier for it.

As he would equally be. Free to choose whomever he wanted and for however long, with no obligation other than what he placed upon himself.

Patrice took a deep, calming breath and stepped into the reach of his arms. Her expressive eyes were tinged with such sadness that he felt compelled to reach out and wrap an arm about her shoulders. She barely came up to his collarbone. Women; so small, so fragile. He did love this one, and he knew she loved him, even when she behaved like an overbearing elder sibling. "I'm sore sorry, I did not mean to bring up bad memories."

"It doesn't matter." She pulled back, shaking off any residue of melancholy.

Perhaps not so fragile after all, he decided. Not Patrice, at least. A myriad of expectations was forced on her, willing or not, and yet she shirked none of them, no matter how much they might impede her own wishes. She was far worthier than him.

Patrice handed over the clothes she had picked. "What *does* matter is that you take a wife. Surely you want a family of your own." Her hazel eyes were inquisitive.

"No, Patrice. I don't." Predilection aside, he would not be responsible for passing his cursed gift along to another generation. If he could, he would have it stop with him.

He felt small arms come around him and peered down to see an innocent face filled with solicitude. "I'll marry you, Merry," Sofie said. "I can't have babies either. If I did, I would die. We can both grow old together and you'll not need to be alone, ever."

Her gentle words broke his heart and he knelt to her level, looking into the old soul that stared back from that young face. Her beautiful cheeks were still chubby, her delicate chin dimpled and her lips, pink, pretty and pouty. She promised to grow into a handsome woman one day, with her rosy-pale skin, so fresh and soft, and her abundant dark-red curls. But her glowing eyes, so different from any Durante, were the most startling.

She knew the pain of a father's neglect, of never being good enough, even if she could not understand the reason.

"No, no, sweet Sofie." He petted her hair and traced her cheek and cried inside at the guilt such a young and impressionable thing carried.

Both he and Patrice had reassured her, and yet Durans Durante's behaviour could only encourage such a belief. If only they were at liberty to enlighten the girl as to his real motivation: that it was not her, but their mother who had turned the man so bitter. But she was a child and not yet mature enough to understand the implications. His and Patrice's love would have to suffice, even if it seemed inadequate.

"You won't die. Your mamma dying when you were born was not your doing, you know that."

Sofie nodded soberly and straightened her shoulders. "Of course I do."

She sounded so sure that Meran wondered from what source the maudlin idea had sprung. Who could know the minds of the young? They were always filled with surprises. Yet his curiosity was piqued, so he asked, "Then how can you know your own fate, sweetheart?"

Looking shy for a moment, a shrug was her only answer.

Patrice tapped him on the shoulder and handed him back the clothes he had dropped. Her look said without words that she would talk with their little sister and get to the bottom of it. He had, after all, more pressing matters to attend to. "Come along, the bathhouse awaits. Take these with you and make haste. Father is waiting."

Meran rolled his eyes and resigned himself. "If I must," he sighed. After all, what choice did he have? Even if he wanted to, he could not ignore the man forever.

He watched as Patrice encouraged Sofie from the room. Still, his heart hurt. Lord Marshal Durans might expect—demand—more of him than he would have liked, but at least he warranted his father's attention. Sofie spent the entirety of her small life without the receipt of any.

CHAPTER TEN

Despite Meran's prompt arrival, his father kept him waiting. It was a tactic no doubt used to increase his agitation and one that Meran knew well. It worked, tension building in every muscle, Meran's stomach roiling as much from the aftermath of too much alcohol as from anxiety.

Whether it proved a bad idea or not, he filled a goblet from a jug on a tray sitting on a side table. Sipping, he flopped himself onto one of the many divans cluttering the dining room. His stomach threatened to object at the first bitter and unappealing taste. He forced more down until the churning stilled. But nothing could quell the turbulence of his mind.

Arguments ran on a continuous loop in his head, justifications for his behaviour falling far short the longer he waited, and yet he could not release his building resentment. He hated the restrictions his father's position placed upon him; the expectations, lack of freedom, the constant scrutiny. For the sake of his own reputation, Meran's father appeared to be happy to have Meran as celibate as one of the temple's many priests. Well, that would never happen. Why deny his appetites when they had proven the only avenue for relief from the threat of the vision? He would not bend to the will of a man whose own lamentable behaviour had lost him the attention of his own wife.

That scandal had set tongues wagging for many a year. Meran did not blame his mother. Lord Marshal Durans was a distant and complicated man and so different from the woman he had married. At this precise moment, Meran could appreciate the overwhelming need for affection and understanding Loreto Melan Tish-Durante must have over the years come to crave more than her honour.

Meran gave the palatial setting surrounding him a withering look. What did the plush furnishings matter? The expensive drapery, the carved filigree adorning the window spaces, the art dressing the walls, the vases and ornamentation cluttering the shelving? His mother had been right to spurn it all to live in a small cottage, even if only to secure herself a dangerous and yet fleeting moment of happiness.

If he had the courage, he would do no less than she. But he felt himself unready. Unready to let go of the hope that he would one day make his father proud. Although today was obviously not that day.

Meran squirmed in his chair, again experiencing the ache left behind by his bawdy behaviour. He did not regret it. Perhaps it had not ensured a full night's relief from the terror of his dreams, but it had given him enough of a reprieve, and for many and varying reasons, he wanted it again.

Like a black cloud, Durans Durante finally strode into the room, Meran having to stop himself from jumping to his feet. Meran forced his features to relax and to sip his wine with mocking contemplation as he took his father in. His behaviour would not placate the man, but the interview threatened to be loud and obnoxious no matter Meran's state of being. He would not have his father know the wait had affected him.

Durans had the flashing, electric-blue eyes of many a Durante, his gaze landing on Meran like a liquid storm. His father's handsome face was pinched with fury.

"You will have the decency to stand when I address you," he bit out, stance wide, hands clasped behind his back as if to stop himself from throttling his heir.

Meran lowered the goblet, his movements slow and deliberate as he stood, awaiting the impending explosion. It came with a solid and resounding slap to his face. The unexpected strike stung equally in his heart as on his cheek, and Meran could not hold back his gasp.

"*Fool boy,*" his father shouted. "Do you know what you have cost me?"

"Your damned pride, no doubt." Meran ducked. For his impudence, the next strike landed against his ear. It smarted with the same heat as the burning on his cheek.

"You will not speak to me so impertinently." His father's face reddened with undeniable rage.

Meran pressed his lips hard together to keep from further protest.

"Not alone did I have to suffer the tale of your outrageous antics from that simpering, fool of a friend of yours, but from Perico, himself!"

Meran's mind blossomed with confusion. *Master Perico?* Why would the man who had given almost as much pleasure to him as Rune Gratian seek out his father to tattletale such intimate detail? Were Gratian and Perico not friends?

His bewilderment must have been writ large all over his face.

"He came this very noon to advise that he would not be taking up my offer for the shipment of his goods. And do you know why?"

What offer? What shipments? Perplexity reigned in Meran's breast. *Who, by the hells, was Paavo Perico to his father?*

"You, that is why," his father answered for him.

Meran gaped.

"I have never witnessed a man so obnoxiously proud of himself," Meran realised his father's anger ran as deep for Paavo as it did for Meran himself. "For months, we have been in negotiations; and at each meeting or dinner invitation has he requested—no, insisted—upon your presence, which I denied him."

"But why? Have you not always wished for me to take an interest—"

"It was not your *interest* in the intricacies of negotiations that he wished to forward! His every intention raised my suspicion, and rightly so, it would seem. I will not barter the virtue of my son to secure a contract.

"But…" Words failed Meran. He did not know what to interject. He felt his own suspicions rise inside his stomach along with the bile of betrayal.

"He came today, to this very house," his father announced, as if that were almost the greater sin, "to tell me Rune Gratian had secured the contract. No doubt because he had been able to facilitate what I would not."

The man had asked his father, Meran's own sire, to offer *him* as an incentive on a business transaction? Horror crashed over Meran. Who would have the gall to even contemplate such a thing? Obviously, Paavo Perico. But why? Before his night at Rune's, Meran had never laid eyes on the man. He had thought Perico's interest a spur of the moment thing; a consequence of the effects of ample drink, good company, and a short-lived desire. But it had been calculated, and all to slack a lust that bordered on disturbing.

Alongside nausea, anger stirred through Meran, and not only for his betrayer. "You can hardly blame me for what I did not know."

"Ignorance is no excuse." His father's scathing tone felled him. "Ellom warned you that the Durante's and Gratian's were at enmity, but he tells me that you refused to listen."

"By the gods, that was not the way of it. Rune"—he noted his father bridle at the familiarity of his use of Gratian's birth name. Refusing to quail, Meran forged on—"offered Jon patronage. Jon needs the money now that his scholarship has run its course and you refused to undertake his patronage yourself. What else could he do? It was a decent offer and he asked me to accompany him to ensure its success. I could not deny him."

"So, you would whore yourself for the sake of your friendship? Have you no pride?"

"It wasn't like that," Meran protested. While he balked at the idea of admitting to his father how much he had fallen under their spell— how he had yielded to their direction and delighted in it—he could not comprehend their tacit betrayal. He had trusted them, especially Rune. Had it all been a horrible deception?

"It was nought but a ruse, you young fool. I doubt Jon will get a penny now. And for your stupidity, we also lose a goodly sum to a man who has sold his soul to trade with that Velkor pirate, The Ballan. Half all profits made from this will go to the Summer Isles, not our own people. *And* we have become a laughingstock! This cannot be endured. No more, Meran. I will have no more of this loose and lewd behaviour from you. From now on, you will give up your rooms and move back here where I can keep an eye on you."

Meran spluttered. "No!" How could the man so callously take away the little freedom he had earned with his acceptance to the prestigious university? "No, *I* pay for that room with the money mother left me. You can't insist on this." But he knew that was not true. Yes, his mother had come from wealth, but anything that had been hers from the dower contract fell under her husband's administrations until her children were of age sufficient to inherit. So far, only Patrice had gained control of her own funds.

"I can and I do insist. You are my son and under my jurisdiction, do you hear me? I have already had the funds in trust to you from that woman stopped, and it will not be released until I see fit. You have until the dinner hour to have your possessions returned to your rooms here. And do not expect to wallow in the sympathy of your friends, I'll have none allowed on my premise until you can prove you have come to your senses. Now get out."

The enormity of it all hit Meran hard, and he floundered like a fish out of water, unable to form a sentence of protest other than to stutter out, "B-but, Father!" at the man's retreating back.

Impotent rage boiled, a small table suffering Meran's expression of it as it flew across the rug, crashing against the tiles with a deafening crack. His feelings unrelieved, Meran swiped the tray from another, the decanter shattering, red wine spraying and food splattering or rolling where it would.

A mirror crashed and a priceless vase smashed, falling victim to his temper, but his father did not return and, unappeased, Meran ran out, determined never to come back.

Fury drove him down streets he barely took note of. Shivering and shaking, his hands clenched and unclenched as rage and despair alternately rode him.

How could his father be so obtuse, and Rune so callous? He could not believe the behaviour of Gratian. To crush his belief, his confidence, in such a flagrant and uncaring manner. The realisation hurt more than he dared to admit. But, then, his father? He was the worst. Punishing him for another's guile and machinations? There was no doubt he was the victim in all of this, his trust so heartlessly exploited.

Rune had known his identity all along. Shame burned with such ferocity. Meran had liked him. He'd liked Rune's generosity, though apparently it was an illusion. He had liked the wisdom that came with the man's maturity. But most of all, he had liked that Rune retained a wild exuberance for intimacy and handled himself with such expertise. Both he and Paavo had built Meran up and made him come over and over again, culminating in the pair of them spreading him and taking him together.

They had used him for their own pleasure, of course he knew that, but through it all they had ensured his willingness. He had revelled in everything they had done to him. But they had lied, not with their bodies, not even their words, but with their intentions. Meran's humiliation swelled, the urge to hit something again undeniable. A harsh whitewashed wall crushed his knuckles, blood splattering and staining its pristine surface.

"*Fuck! Fuck! Fuck!*" The agony bloomed so brilliant he could hardly speak as he clutched his hand to his chest and cursed himself for a mindless fool. Turning, he backed to the wall and slid down the rough surface to land on the cobbled pavement. Tears streamed his cheeks from more than the pain.

"Son, are you ill?"

The voice made him jump. Opening his bleary eyes, he stared into a familiar visage. She was diminutive, like her son, but of everything else, Ellom had only inherited the grey eyes of his mother. She had ringlets of strawberry blonde, a gamine expression, with a pointed chin. She looked not a day over fifty, having been an infamously young bride.

She had caused quite the scandal, being Meran's own age when Ellom, her eldest, was born. In comparison, Meran's own mother had been threescore and ten at Beorn's birth and had exceeded her first century by twenty years at his. That was the norm for those of *Vocekind*.

"Mistress Marius?" Meran cast a hasty scan of the scenery, shocked at where he found himself. The very blood-spattered wall to his back was that which surrounded Ellom's parent's estate. He could not believe that despite his anger with the lad, he found himself here. What had drawn him to this spot, he did not know, but Meran feared he could not understand his own mind let alone know what to say to this woman.

"Come, dear boy," Mistress Marius said, looking him over, she urged him to his feet. "You look dazed; and that cut extremely nasty." She referred to his hand. "Come inside. Ellom is from home and I've not a clue where he is. But I'm sure he will be back if you've come to call."

Meran tried to shake his head clear even as she tucked herself beneath his arm—as if her small frame had any hope of supporting him—and led him along the line of the fence to a side gate. She took him down a path that curved around a flat grassed area and into a small cloister thick with kitchen herbs and a tinkling fountain.

"There's a chamber where you may rest for the healing of that," Mistress Marius said, leading him into the house proper and a maze of rooms. Servants quarters most like, but the one she entered with him in tow boasted more than a simple chaise and stool. It held a broad-cushioned divan, satin-stitched quilt in soft cream, a brocaded footstool of golden thread, carved side table, and matching padded chest that served as a seat.

"I thank you, ma'am." Meran lowered himself down where she directed.

"Oh, think nothing of it. The girls are from home visiting an aunt, and I find myself at a loose end." She cast him a curious glance as he settled back. "Were you attacked?" she enquired. "Shall I call for the constabulary?"

"It's nought, nought," he hastened to assure her. "I'll heal it and rest a little and then be on my way." He did not wish to confront Ellom. Not at this juncture, when his fury ruled, and his emotions were beyond his control. He might say or do something they would both regret, even if he felt Ellom deserved his censure. Not for being right, but for having gone behind his back to inform his father.

"Of course, dear. I'll have one of the maids bring you a drink and some cheese for the healing's aftermath."

The pain from his injury throbbed through him, flaring with even the most minuscule of movement. As soon as she left, he set his healing magic to work, despite the fact it would leave him asleep and vulnerable once accomplished. While with the lord's family in Atena his eyes had been opened to the misery that those who were not *Voce* suffered when injured. The expending of a little energy and the rejuvenating sleep that followed was a small price to pay for immediate healing. He was grateful for Mistress Marius' hospitality, too, though it left him with a small debt for her generosity.

When he awoke, the woman herself, not the promised maid, sat pensively beside the divan, candles placed strategically about the darkened room.

Meran sat up, his knuckles healed but his chest tightening. At first, apprehension flooded him that he may have missed his new curfew. Following on its heels, resentment flamed to life that at his age, he had even been given one at all. *Gods damn his father.* Let the bastard stew.

Gratefully, he took the drink, bunch of grapes, and sticks of cheese from Mistress Marius' hand. As his mind cleared, a frown furrowed his brow in concern for her presence. "Is everything well?" he asked.

Her expression creased with worry. "I'm uncertain," she began. "When did you last see my Ellom?"

Meran grimaced. "Last eve before his dinner with the committee." But he was more than obviously not the last one to see him. "He visited the lord marshal's."

"Pray, when was this?"

Meran shook his head, realising his father had not mentioned the details of Ellom's visit. "Did he not return to tell you if he'd had any success with the faculty members?"

Mistress Marius' deep grey eyes shone with a hollow glimmer. "He did not, and each hour I grow more concerned. It is not like him. Ellom is a good boy."

Boy, he most definitely was not, but who could persuade a mother that their child would invariably grow up or be anything but good? "I'm sure he's fine," he tried to reassure her. Yet, Ellom's feelings of fury with him were as likely a match for Meran's own. No doubt he now attempted to avoid Meran's company after what he had done. "Have you sought him out with the farsight?"

Almost as soon as he'd said it, Meran knew he sounded a fool.

"I've tried, as have the servants," she assured without censure.

Of course she would have used it. The farsight was a gift inherent in all of *Vocekind*. It was a gift that allowed their people to see with their minds rather than their eyes. Yet it had its limitations, stone being a major impediment. The buildings of *Voce* were not built of or lined with stone for nothing, it being the only substance known to ensure privacy from the power of the ability.

A tear trembled on the brink of Mistress Marius' lashes and her lips quivered. "His father is to Cora's Island and not due for home until the next full moon."

Even if he wanted to cling to his own hurt and anger, pity for the lone woman forced Meran to set aside his own feelings for himself. This woman was no Patrice. She looked so forlorn, as innocent and fragile as young Sofie. "Here, let me try," Meran said, as if he would succeed where she had failed. He doubted his magic was superior. The distance a man on horseback could travel in three days was the limit of his talent. But Ellom had to be somewhere within that radius.

With the woman by his side, Meran returned to the street. Though the Marius' townhouse and gardens were substantial, they were situated closer to the docks than Meran's family's. Standing just outside the gates, the sounds of the port floated in on the breeze, and along with it came the hum of a night filling with activity.

Though he did not need to, Meran shut his eyes and let the magic open to him. Conjuring the image of Ellom in his mind should have had the sight find him immediately. Instead, he found nothing.

Meran sent his farsight sweeping to and fro, crisscrossing the landscape. He noted the dead aura of dirt and stone and the glow of life from the abundant vegetation of the port city's many gardens. He observed the radiant emanations of life force flowing from both animals and people as they went about their business. Some came to him clearly, images of those he knew or had seen in real life. The others were a rainbow of colours, but in all that, he saw no sign of his infuriating friend.

He tried again with the same result.

"You see nought either." Mistress Marius began to cry softly.
Trying to hide his perturbation, Meran took her hand. "Have no fear, Mistress," he said. "I'll round up the lads and we will mount a search. No doubt he's with friends at the Petrel's End and has forgotten the time." Meran swallowed. He did not believe his own assertions. He and Ellom had mutual friends, and he had spied them in various locations about the city. Ellom was with none of them. So where could he possibly be?

CHAPTER ELEVEN

Three days later and Meran was beside himself with worry. Ellom still had not been found.

Of their small family, all but their father sat about the atrium. Patrice ate nibbles of raw vegetables dipped in a combination of whipped cheese and spices. Sofie played in the water that channelled around the outside of the square drain at the room's centre. Getting her hair and the front of her dress wet, Sofie leaned over to splash at the circling fish, the sun streaming through the open roof turning her coppery-red curls to fire. The small moat was one of the many examples of extravagance that populated the lord marshal's house.

"Damn the man!" Meran cursed his sire.

He lay sprawled on a bench, arms thrown over his face to hide his frustration. "He hinders me at every turn," he said. "This is too important; can't he see that?"

"I imagine if you'd adhered to father's curfew, or even came to him for his aid, you would not have been led back home like a recalcitrant child and so would not now be in this position."

Patrice's observation did little to placate Meran. He threw her a terse look. "He should not have sent the law after me. It was meant only to embarrass me. I did not attempt to hide. He knew where I was, and what I was doing. I could feel his gaze on me every moment after leaving Ellom's mother. But damn him still! There is much more need for me to help with the search, even now."

"I'm not sure it would make any difference," she answered. "Do you know how many fellows are out there, prowling the landscape? Fifty good men, and still they are eluded. Do you know what that says to me?"

"I know, I know," Meran said, despite his wont, he had come to the same conclusion. "He does not wish to be found. But I don't understand why."

To his immense irritation, Patrice kept her own counsel. To Meran, her thoughts were obvious. She suspected his own behaviour the cause. And as much as he wanted to deny the supposition, he feared she was right.

Meran flung himself from his seat at the injustice and began to pace back and forth until Sofie flicked water on him as he passed. "You must ask the old man," she told him in all seriousness.

"What old man?" he asked, barely listening and distractedly brushing the beads of water from his breeches as he carried on along his course.

"The old man in the clouds."

"Such an imagination." Patrice smiled indulgently at their sister.

Sofie's large fiery eyes lifted, admonishing them both. "No," she said. "I see him in my dreams. He waves at me sometimes and speaks, but I mostly can't hear him. There are clouds that always get in the way should I move too close. But I know he wants to talk to me and show me things."

Patrice and Meran exchanged a puzzled look. "What does the old man look like, Sofie?" Meran asked.

"Well, his hair is ever so white—not like yours, Merry, yours is moonbeam—his is *old* white and long—even longer than Patty's! And he has crinkles all over his face. I think he must be as old as the gods. But he is nice," she added as if comparing him to the gods would make them think otherwise. "He plays in the water, too. Not a silly little pool like this, but a big river, full of magic."

Meran stifled a bemused laugh to cover his rising concern and came to a halt, crouching at her side. "Sofie, sweetheart." He captured her chin with the tips of his fingers. "How often do you see this man?"

She smiled as if bringing his visage to the fore of her mind. "Most nights when I have the ghost dreams."

"Ghost dreams?"

She laughed. "You know. The ghost dreams, silly! I come out of myself, but I'm not scared… well, I was to start, but the thread keeps me safe even when I'm light as a cloud. I look funny, and the wind blows right through me, and I float, but I don't fly away. Most of the time there are people I can hear, but they are too far away to see. It makes me sad. You need to have a ghost dream and ask the old man to show you where your friend is. I think that's the only way you'll find him."

Meran threw Patrice a helpless look and noted the stark paleness of her face. "So soon," she said, horror dawning across her expression.

Ignoring the sinking feeling in his stomach, he turned back to his little sister. "I never see the old man in th-the ghost dreams, Sofie."

Sofie turned back to the poor fish and continued splashing vigorously. "He's there. You just need to call him. I did hear him last eve—he said your name. His face was all grumpy like Da's. He *really* wants to talk to you, Merry, but you're always watching the dying man."

Meran stalled, his mouth dropping open. *By the gods!* What were these dreams Sofie had, and even more importantly, how could she know of Beorn? Sofie had never even had the chance to meet her older brother.

Meran swallowed the lump in his throat. At that moment, he did not want to be reminded of Beorn, either. He shut down his memories and chose the distraction. Surely this old man that Sofie thought she saw should command his attention. "What does he want to say, and how can I call him if I don't know his name?" he asked.

"He's called Fido."

"Fido?"

Sofie screwed her face up again, thinking hard. "Mayhap not Fido. I'm sorry, Merry, I try to hear but..." A tear sparkled at the edge of her eye as if her not knowing meant that she had somehow failed Meran.

"No, no. It is well, my sweet, you mustn't fret," he soothed. *Gods balls,* he was an arse. It was probably nothing. She was too young, wasn't she? This was unprecedented. But, knowing her lineage, what if it was not as unprecedented as he might think? What if this was important, this man who called to his little sister? "Close your eyes and if you can, try to find the sounds in your memory. They begin with *fff*?"

Doing as bid, Sofie's lips parted, *"Fffidlo? Fillo? Filo...?"*

A thought struck, accompanied by the memory of musty old books and, in particular, one large tome. "Philo? Do you mean Philo, as in Philo Janiusz?"

"Oh, yes! That's it." She nodded, her face brightening with relief at his guess. It was a confirmation that stunned both him and Patrice, from the sound of her gasp. And one that shook Meran to the very core of his beliefs.

"Sweetheart, Philo Janiusz is the name of a prophet and he's been dead for a very, very, very long time."

"I know," she said simply, as if the man's passing did not matter a jot. "So he'll *have* to know where your friend is. He can see everything from heaven, can't he? I'm sure he'll tell you and then your heart won't have to hurt anymore."

Meran shuddered at the simplicity of her childish intuition. He did worry: His heart did hurt. Feelings of guilt had a tenacious grip, that much he knew.

But how, at her tender age, could she have even heard the prophet's name? Of course, he was inextricably part of *Voce* mythology, but most tutors and philosophers thought the collection of his prophecies the scratchings of a once-revered man gone mad.

Mostly referred to as The Prophet, all credited him with the rescuing of the first people at the reeving of the Etherworld; of taking them through the glistening gate that had broken them down and refashioned them into the beings they were now; endowed with magic. The Prophet had led this new breed of humanity to this land they had named Locurnia—Place of Rest—but the cost had been his own sanity.

How could Meran reconcile this version of Philo with what his little sister now so innocently proclaimed? And, more importantly, even if it were true, how would he be able to connect with Philo's spirit? Meran could not force himself into a trance. Even in his current state of exhaustion, sleep continued to elude him.

And, should sleep finally come, what then? If the *ghost dreams* deigned to come, he had never had one jot of control over them. They led him where they would; ever to Beorn and the fatal conflict that played out at the very verge of that strange island in the midst of Aleia. His visions were trapped there, and he unable to break free. Meran returned to his couch and flopped down. Covering his face, he groaned into his hands.

He felt a tender touch brushing his hair from his forehead and lowered his hands to look into big concerned eyes. "Don't worry, Merry," Sofie said. "I can stay with you if you want. I can get the feather and you can make snow again. I won't let Patty wake you this time, so when the old man reaches for you, you can take his hand."

Meran stared in absolute bemusement. *The snow, how could she even know of it?* The *Voce's* true magic only manifested itself at puberty, and she was a child barely beyond the years of weaning. How could she intuit so much? But then, Sofie was not fully his blood. Was it as he suspected? That this confounding ability came from the mixing of seer blood through their mother's line and the potency inherent in Sofie's father's? He had no one to ask.

Meran knew the mingling had been exceptional, the relationship dangerous and ultimately deadly. For a moment, he understood his own sire's hesitancy to connect with such a child. But Meran knew Durans Durante was wrong. There was something amazing and unique in his little sister, and above all else, this talent needed nurturing.

Meran sat up and gently took the girl by the shoulders, looking into her dark amber eyes. He asked with soft intention, "What do you mean, 'make snow'?"

Her smile broadened, her tone carefree. "*You* made the snow."

"I made the snow?"

"Of course! You remember when Da took us all to the mountains and it snowed, and we played in it?"

"I do." Though how she remembered, Meran did not know. She had been little more than a babe of two and tied to his back in a leather carrying sack. Covered in furs, only her nose and a few strands of her wayward curls popped out from beneath her hood. Yet, he remembered her squeals of delight. Her kicking feet. The flush of chill-pink that had rosied her cheeks as the flakes had danced over them, tickling their skin with cold fairy kisses.

"The feather made you remember," she said. "Just do that again."

CHAPTER TWELVE

Meran was struck dumb. His little sister thought it so simple, but it was far from it. He did not know how the feather had translated into the snow in his mind, nor did he know how remembering it had released him from his prison. He did not even know what kept him shackled to the one vision in the first place. If he did, he would do all within his power to break free of it, but he could not.

"Sofie, sweetheart," Patrice interrupted his churning thoughts. "I would have you return my platter to the kitchens and ask Missy for a pitcher of cider. I trust you to be careful in bringing it back for me and Merry. Can you do that?"

Sofie cast Meran a knowing glance as if the child saw through Patrice's ruse to secure a moment to themselves. To his surprise, his little sister did not make a fuss.

"Of course," Sofie said, and taking the plate Patrice held out, she skipped away without a backward glance.

A niggling fear wormed its way through Meran's belly at the thought of the conversation that would now follow. Patrice's expression, a fusion of pity, curiosity, and resolution, told him she was determined to get to the bottom of the matter. Little dissuaded her when her mind was thus set.

The sudden dread of what might be revealed if Patrice continued along this course, made him shudder. Unfounded or not, he feared that what held him back would be revealed as a weakness all his own, a flaw intrinsic to his character, and he did not know if he could live with such a failing. Anxiety almost forced him to his feet and away from her compelling hazel gaze.

"Will it work?" she asked, getting to the point. "What Sofie has said, will it free you from the vision of this dying man? Will you be able to look for Ellom?"

"N-no." Shame coloured Meran's cheeks. He would fail even when so much of import rode upon his success. "It won't work. It can't."

How could it work when he was ignorant? But, no longer could he run from his magic if he wanted to help. Running was all it seemed he had ever done since the first time he had experienced the call of the dreamlands. *Oh, what would he not give for a mentor!* he mourned. *To have someone who knew what they were doing could only prove a balm for his very soul!*

"How do you know until you try?" Patrice asked.

Of course she had no idea of the complexity. "You don't understand."

"No, I don't, but what other choice is there?" she demanded. "If you don't, what will happen to Ellom?"

"I don't know." Meran's exasperation grew. At himself, at her for expecting more of him than he could give. "No, no. I just can't…" To choose to see that vision, even in the throes of trying to overcome it, smacked of masochism.

"Why? Tell me." They glared at each other, Patrice's lips finally pressing into a pinched line. "Never did I take you for a coward, brother."

Indignation flared at her accusation. "I'm not a coward. I am just not the seer everybody wants me to be. I see nothing of value, only the same thing over and over and over."

But was it cowardice? What would really become of him if he chose to let the vision of Beorn pass? Even in the depths of his despair, seeing that loved and loathed face meant more to Meran than he could stand. For his brother to be lost to him forever? It was unthinkable. As a child, Meran had idolised Beorn until death tore him away and left him alone and with a responsibility he could not fulfil. So why couldn't he let go?

"And that vision?" Patrice leaned towards him, hand outstretched to touch his, voice soft and pleading. "Will you tell me what it is? Who the dying man is?"

"I wouldn't dare share such torment with you." Meran pulled back from her touch. He had only ever confessed the truth of the vision to his father, back when it had first come upon him. Somehow, it had become too personal. Beorn; his nemesis, his desolation; *his, his, his.* Being now the only one privileged enough to see it, he owned that vision and would let none other touch it. Jealousy billowed in his breast in the wake of her request, and the truth stabbed at him. *Ye gods!* Did he truly savour this misery despite how he thought to run away from it?

"Why, Meran. Why won't you let me share this burden?"

His sister, always so well put together.

"I am only trying to hel—"

"I see Beorn," he interrupted, his voice cracking, his face heating, his words sharp with the effort to release the dark secret and see her quail in shock. Her horrified expression turned out not to be the catharsis he had hoped for. It did not take long for her to overcome her initial surprise.

He swallowed. "I-I see him in Aleia." Still, his voice broke, a well of emotion shattering loose. Sorrow clogged his throat as he remembered Beorn's familiar face, his eyes still alive and brilliant. "Again and again and again, I see him. I see the creatures overwhelm his patrol. I see their darts stab into his neck. I see the paralysis that claims him, and then…"

Tears broke free, flowing down Meran's cheeks as he crumpled with the release of his burden.

"Oh, sweetheart," Patrice crooned, tears glistening in her own eyes. "Tell me."

"You don't want to know," he whispered.

"But I do." She shook her head, sliding along the seat, her arms grasping about him, the firmness of her hold speaking of her compassion and support. "I want to be by your side, to bear it with you. Dear, sweet Merry, please will you let me?"

Her consolation wrecked him. She offered an ear if only to halve his burden. Not pity, but love. Whether it would help, Meran could not tell; but need drove him towards confession, a liberating outpouring of the wound that plagued his dreams.

"T-they c-cut him down. Blades to his chest, his throat." He gasped a hitching breath. Anger bloomed, laced with desperation. "You would think my heart would be hardened by the repetition, but it is not. It grows ever weaker. More and more it tears me up until I am a blathering mess. I boil with fury and despair, both in equal measure. I am shattered every time the light leaves his eyes and I want to scream at him, '*why do you have to be there?*' I was a child. And he… he was everything to me."

"I know, I know."

Patrice stroked his hair, and Meran let it soothe him until his turmoil settled a little. He scrubbed the worst of his tears from his face. "I worshipped the ground on which his feet trod," he admitted.

The understanding in her eyes told him that she already knew. "And he loved you as only a big brother can."

Yes, he had. Beorn had loved him, and that only made it worse. Meran remembered the bear hugs, the mock battles, the swordplay with his little wooden blades so minuscule in Beorn's big hands. The camping expeditions, the quiet moments when Beorn had told him tales of glory, and the game of Nine Men that Beorn had deigned to play with him. His brother had given so freely of his time and his heart. Even though Meran now knew the man had shouldered many a responsibility, he had never ignored Meran, until... "He left me."

"They all did," Patrice excused. "They had to."

"I know. But he didn't come back." That constituted his brother's greatest sin. "Why could he not have been one of those who survived? He is ten times the worth of those that did!" Meran could say that with all certainty. He had experienced the arrogance and manipulation of those who had survived first-hand.

"The war took both the good and the bad," she said, her tone sombre.

"Oh, you dare to wax philosophical with me at this time?" Meran tried to tease to lighten the constriction in his heart, the same emotion he saw reflected on Patrice's face.

She smiled at his attempt and mussed his hair with affection. "Only if it is the truth."

Quiet descended while Meran warred with his own truth, hesitant to admit it to himself, let alone to say it out loud. It squirmed in his belly, aching to be free. "I can't forgive him," he finally said. "I can never forgive him for what he did."

"My sweet love." Patrice knelt between his knees on the tiles and took his face between her palms. "You have to. I see now why you are stuck in this one place. But what has come to pass cannot be held against Beorn. You must not torture yourself with it. He did only what was best, what was expected of every able man in the king's service. He did it to save our people from a fate that could not be endured. Without his sacrifice and the sacrifices of all those that lost their lives, Locurnia and all those that you know would be no more."

Guilt and anger swirled like a maelstrom, but Meran recognised his own selfishness. Beorn's absence had spawned a situation that he could neither accept for himself nor bear when he failed. "I can't do it. I just can't," he said. "He should be here. He should be here to follow in father's footsteps. Beorn; the one everybody expected, loved, and wanted. I am not him. You see father's disappointment in me—how he treats me. There is no fire in my soul for the position Beorn has left me. His shoes… they are impossible for me to fill."

A look of surprise flashed in Patrice's eyes and Meran realised how pathetic he sounded. Their brother was dead, their world at peace, and he cared only that he was now forced to be the heir of Durans Durante. Patrice and he had conversed on this subject many a time, and each time he had sensed her growing impatience with him. Still, her words when they came were firm and composed. "No, you are not Beorn, that is true; but never think that he was always as you remember. You were a child, and he had done a lot of growing up before you ever came into this world. Father is going nowhere soon. You will have the same opportunity to grow as he did."

Meran offered her a dubious look. Should he be offended that she inferred he behaved like a child? He had always considered himself mature and intelligent, even if that came liberally salted with a desire for frivolity.

"You think you are wild?" Patrice laughed, memories dancing behind her eyes. "To Beorn, you do not hold a candle."

Meran huffed his disbelief.

"Let me tell you, Beorn's behaviour had Father beside himself many a time."

It was all Meran could do to stop his mouth from hanging open. "Pray, what? Are you saying, he and father clashed?"

Her brow raised pointedly. "Indeed—loudly and often. And just like you, Beorn refused to heed him. So often Father feared that there would be at least a dozen little bastards seeking the Durante name. Only luck, not prudence on our brother's part, kept that from coming to pass."

Meran's doubtful laughter followed her confession. "Surely you are not saying he was another Jon?"

Patrice quirked a brow and she resumed her seat by his side. "I think perhaps not. He did not run with those of your persuasion."

Meran cleared his throat. "Jon does not exactly *run* with us either, in that regard."

"Hmm." She offered him a sceptical look.

Meran sighed. While he knew her to be wrong when it came to Jon, that Beorn had not always been the competent leader he remembered made his head spin. The strong, vigilant, valiant, and caring man he thought he knew, had been a rake? A revelation, indeed.

"Why did you not tell me this before?" he demanded.

Patrice ignored his tone of accusation. "When would I have either had the opportunity or the inclination? We were both in mourning for our mother, and I, a child to rear. Before the change came upon you, you were a child yourself and the subject unbroachable. And then you had your studies." Patrice shrugged. "When would have been appropriate? Tell me."

He gave a short laugh. He could have wished for such knowledge while entangled in every altercation with his father, but she could not have known his need of it until this moment. "Now," he answered. But did this new knowledge change anything? He did not know.

"Aye," Patrice said. "Now, should you attempt this thing, as I think you must"—At her words, his heart dropped—"do you think the spectre of Beorn will still hold you captive?"

"I-I don't know. I know so little." He shook his head. "I don't know if my feelings were even the reason for my captivity." Although he now suspected that they played a major part. With his confession and his tears and the knowledge that Beorn had not been the epitome of perfection, he felt some of the consuming weight lift from his shoulders. There was still a fist of grief about his heart, but its grasp was now not so tight. Perhaps, if he could indeed let it go... "Sofie may say as much as she will that I can *do that again*, but I certainly don't know if I have the wherewithal to make the dreamlands snow at my whim, nor what to do after. And that's before considering how I could even gain access to that plane when sleep evades me."

"Ah." Patrice looked thoughtful, her gaze swinging towards Sofie as the little girl walked sedately into the room with a chilled jug on a silver tray. Light sparkled in his older sister's dark eyes. "Speaking of Jon," she said. "I think I have an idea. Sofie dearest, I thank you for the drink, but now I have another message for you to give Missy, if you would."

CHAPTER THIRTEEN

"So," Jon said. "He offered me a thousand shirls."

They were seated in a small alcove to the rear of the villa, carved marble bench beneath their buttocks and slate tiles beneath their feet. There was stone enough to obstruct his father's farsight and a sufficient abundance of creepers to hinder any other unwanted scrutiny.

"Who?" Meran asked, but he already knew. It had to be Rune, and the amount proffered Jon, a small fortune.

"Gratian," Jon confirmed. "But after what he and that degenerate did, I would not touch it with the longest oar that came to hand."

Meran's face blazed that even Jon should know his shame. But the offer? It smacked of an ill-judged attempt at an apology on Rune Gratian's part, or perhaps guilt. Well, until such expression of regret was made to his face, Meran was not predisposed to forgive, and maybe not even then. However, he was still unhappy that his friend could not benefit from the resultant generosity.

Jon's appearance was a little more rumpled than usual. Not stained with the white powder nor smears of charcoal that Meran was used to, but with the grime and unrelenting dry dust of the streets.

"You should have taken it and be damned," he said. "You could have done a lot with that coin."

"And would you still speak to me if I had? I think not." Jon paused, his look undecided. "He gave me a missive for you—"

"Burn it, I would not read it if you paid me." Not because of the humiliation or regret. If he could he would have the mortification of that part of his life over and done. But because he would not let himself wallow in it. Not ever.

"No fear of that," Jon said with dry amusement. "I am once again a starving artist, sucking off the teat of friendship."

A twinge of guilt again sparked through Meran as he looked at the little bag of hampr in his hand. Patrice must have given Jon the coin for its purchase, and perhaps more for the errand. For his friend's status to be so reduced to that of little more than a pauper, and at the Durante's making, sent shame flooding through Meran. "We'll think of something," he reassured.

As always, Jon smiled as if unconcerned by his situation. As if landing on the streets did not bother him. But then, his expression sobered. "I think he is sorry, you know. More than he realised he would be."

Still, Meran refused to take the sealed parchment, even if he suffered a pang of regret when Jon repocketed the unread note. That part of his life was over. He would now keep his trust to himself, where it belonged.

"I swear on my honour, I will fix this," Meran promised. Though he still had no clue how, nor what coin Jon would need to get him from his predicament and on the road to fortune. Now that Jon's tenure at the university was over, Meran did not even know if he had a room to call his own, nor how Missy had come to find him.

"You do not have to," Jon said, shrugging off the offer. "It was not you who reneged. Nor did you prove yourself to be careless or mercenary."

"That doesn't matter. I have played my part, to my shame," Meran said, his determination as staunch as his regret was rife. "And if I could, I would foot the bill myself, but... well, the Durante's have connections and I'm sure someone can be persuaded to see that such talent as yours should not be thrown away on the whims of callous, unthinking men."

Jon's gaze turned thoughtful and Meran could only hope that he would not continue to object. He needed to do this. To try to make up for the harm that had befallen the man due to Meran's own dismal behaviour. That Jon had turned down such a sum could only have him wallowing in regret, though he hid it well.

"If you must," Jon agreed, and Meran's spirits lightened a little.

They sank into a companionable silence.

Finally, Jon plucked the pouch from Meran's fingers. "Are you going to use that?" he asked, at the same time drawing out a smooth, dark-wood pipe from a bag hung about his waist and hidden by his loose tunic. It was what Jon had come for, after all.

Meran's stomach twisted.

Do that again… Do. That. Again!

Sofie's words whirled around and around in Meran's head. If he tried and failed, he would find himself lost to the wiles of the dreamland, unable to pull himself free until the effects of the drug had faded from his mind. Could he stand the montage of death and destruction it would throw his way?

Ignorant of Meran's trepidation, Jon cleared the bowl of the pipe and began packing it with the hampr.

Meran watched, mesmerized by the simple procedure. He fought down his panic. Was he really going to attempt this for the sake of a young man that had denounced him, and who likely wished not to be found?

Yet the memories that taunted him were not of betrayal, but of an earnest, eager face. They were of a friend's excitement in life, their comradery, and their mutual experiences. Mostly, they were of a voice that had commanded and calmed him, and offered him relief the like he had never experienced before.

Ellom might not wish to be discovered, but what if that were not the case? In the name of their long friendship, Meran had to find out.

Rousing himself from his disgruntled reveries, he asked, "By the bye, how in all the hells did you manage to get past my father?" It had not taken Missy long before she came to find Meran with the news that his friend awaited him in the rear arbour.

"The very endearing waif you sent my way smuggled me in through the cellar's rear entrance. She's a pretty wee thing, if I may say," Jon said with a leer.

Meran snorted. The girl had a bust proportionate to a cow's udder, even if the rest of her remained petite. He trusted that Jon had noticed.

"I'm sure she did not give you the time of day," he managed to scoff, glad of the distraction.

Jon smirked. "You'd be surprised." All the while he fiddled with a hemp wick, setting it alight with the lamp Meran had remembered to bring.

"That I would. Patrice sent her, specifically, as she's newly pledged and invulnerable to your allure."

"Then, best her new beau keep a wary eye on her. She's nought but a minx and her sneaky kisses were more than sweet. I may have to mind my own virtue on the return journey."

Meran grumbled, wondering how many of the lasses the man had gone through now. Jon had to do little more than smile and turn his stormy grey eyes upon them and they became simpering messes. They succumbed to the man's rakish charms so easily it was disgusting, and such a waste.

"By the gods, can't you leave the servants be? You will only incur the wrath of my sire should one of them fall to your wiles and get big with child. Do you want to be forced to wed?"

His friend shuddered. "It was only a few kisses, I assure, but point taken." Changing the subject, Jon held the pipe and burning wick aloft. "Right, are we ready?"

He brought the pipe to his own lips and the flame to the dried, packed herbs and drew in a breath. He dragged it back, swirling the smoke about his mouth as if to taste and then breathed it out in a puff, filling the air with the hampr's distinctive aroma.

To Meran's surprise, Jon took a further puff and leaned over and gently blew it beneath Meran's nose. He drew it in until he had little capacity to take any more. It swirled in a hot, smoky rush through the back of his throat and filled his lungs.

Smiling, Jon leaned against the stone block wall at the arbour's back and drew in another deep drag.

They sat, sharing the pipe until the herbs burnt out. Meran shut his eyes and let the hampr do its work.

The evening light danced over the back of his lids as the foliage about the arbour fluttered in a light breeze. He followed the flickering red-and-black susurrations and taking one last slow, calming breath, allowed himself to sink into darkness.

Black boiled back to reveal thick grey and white storm clouds. The shadows of a dense jungle overwhelmed him. The trills and hoots of a myriad of unknown beasts and the buzz of brightly coloured insects assailed his ears… Again, beneath it all, the hubbub of fighting and dying rolled closer; louder. He had no chance to think, the familiarity dragging at him.

Rising like a sun cresting the horizon, the encompassing dome of power that encapsulated Ustra's isle beyond the boiling river filled Meran's vision. Men scattered like ants as the creatures came for them.

Meran followed that familiar flash of blond hair as his brother shouted a retreat. The dark forests swallowed Meran himself as effectively as it swallowed Beorn and his men, and Meran stood paralysed, his heart beating a frantic tattoo as his brother went down.

Tears streamed his cheeks as darts flew and Beorn lay, eyes wide, fingers spasming until they went still. The creatures swarmed.

Pain stabbed at Meran's heart, familiar and soul-destroying. He did not know how he could go on, despair threatening to swamp him, his mind pinned to the dying man and awaiting Beorn's last breath.

As always, Meran wanted to run, but to turn aside now would never save him from the sight of Beorn's death. Until Meran confronted his pain and let go of his sorrow, it would never release him. He could not let cowardice rule him. Not this time.

His simulacrum descended, as if from the sky, to land alongside the prone figure. All but one of the creatures scattered, as if they suddenly sensed his presence. The last crouched with blade to the paralysed man's throat, awaiting the immutable moment it would be drawn across the vulnerable flesh. It must happen, for it had already happened.

Meran sank to his knees in the pooling blood and grasped for his brother's hand, warmth seeping through their connection. His tear-blurred gaze latched to Beorn's face and those brilliant eyes, still so alive and churning. Not with fear. For the first time, Meran saw anger burning in their blue depths. Fury fierce and indefatigable for an enemy who showed no mercy. All about him, his men died, and Beorn raged at his impotence to save them, to vanquish his foes. He loved his men and died abhorring their loss.

Leaning closer, Meran stroked Beorn's hair, as if to free the streaked and dirty blond locks from behind Beorn's ear, surprised at how real his brother felt beneath his touch. "Fear not," he whispered, his voice thick and his throat tight. "Their death, your death, was not in vain. The king, he saved us all. The ophidian were put in their place, brother mine, and none who fought for our king and our victory will ever be forgot. I promise you."

It could have been nothing more than his own imagination, but Beorn's eyes seemed to flicker upward, a glisten of recognition filling them. Meran gasped in surprise. "Beorn, please…"

His heart trembled with all he needed to say, even though he knew this could not be real. Meran had never been in Aleia. Still, Beorn's eyes watched him as the creature's blade bit slowly and surely through his flesh, and the first spray of blood seeped through a wound that would prove fatal.

But what choice had Beorn had? Without question, Meran too

would have answered their king's call. And here in these most final of moments, he had but a second to say the only thing that still needed to be said. "Peace Beorn... I f-forgive you. Farewell, my brother."

Meran stood as his brother breathed out his last, a rattle of liquid air. It was over.

And yet, Meran still found himself captured in the vision as the creatures frenzied in victory. His heart sank. He had meant every word he had said to Beorn. Why was he still suffering this affront?

Think of the feather, remember the snowflakes.

Is that what he must do to break free of this vision once and for all? To secure his own passage through the dreamscape, as he had never done before... to accept his lot and take back control?

Snow. Remember the snow.

Meran closed his ears to the clamour and listened for the hushed sounds of the soft flakes falling. He tuned every sense, every desperate desire, to detecting their delicate dance.

Please...

In this place he had no body, he did not breathe, and yet a breath fluttered over him, a descending chill. Meran opened his eyes to see the sky teeming with the delicate falling clumps and let out a silent exclamation of delight. Snow whirled in dervishes, the wind picked up...

His relief rushed unchecked and the impending storm peeled back as if blown from existence.

Meran found himself at the edge of a clifftop, like the gigantic prow of a ship forging its way through a foreign seascape. It stretched out before him in threads of dark green and billowing grey. Mists, pregnant with water. The distant calls of the jubilant snake people echoed liked the rasp and hum of insects, too small to affect him.

Above, a black sky twinkled with the pinpoints of stars. It was the closest thing to the now that he had ever seen. They held no time, only space and infinite leagues of freedom... Throwing his head back, he rejoiced in his success. Here in the dreamlands, and in a gleaming simulacrum, he was now himself.

Finding his voice, he bellowed out ecstatic hoots of victory again and again and shook his fists at the vision far below his feet, no longer holding him captive. With nothing left to do, he called out.

"Philo Janiusz. I am here."

Breath fluttered warm across the back of his neck, lifting his hair and ruffling the very substance of his naked shade.

"Come, Meran Durante, heir of the most holy seeress, Linette Tish. Welcome to the Plains of Elysia."

Jerked from his feet, his shade flew into the sky and into a tumult of black rushing waters.

"Make your wish and see what the River of Time will reveal unto you."

Unlike Sofie, he could not see anyone, and soon he felt no one's presence. Alone, he paddled in a turbulent current. Jagged stones cut the surface of the unknown river, water foaming around them. The bubbles rushed towards Meran. As they drew near, he could see into their depths, small snippets of lives captured beneath their sheer, shimmering, gossamer skins.

One headed straight for him, holding night, dry darkness, and a familiar body. *El!* He leapt for it, breaking its surface, and found himself tumbling into its depths with a frightened and yet determined cry.

CHAPTER FOURTEEN

"Why would the young master bother coming here?" one of the militiamen grumbled. "'Tis a wild goose chase, you mark me."

"He's a seer," Jon answered curtly, gesturing at Meran, to which the soldier made a rude noise.

Meran could understand his scepticism. The tombs on Silentes Mount were dotted across a dark and densely clad slope that presented itself all the more macabre in the silver moon's band of fading pale light.

No one would come here of their own volition. The caves with their stone-capped entrances, more to keep the spectres in than potential graverobbers out, presented a funereal and joyless landscape. But Meran knew he was right.

Still, he regretted that the biggest and most prominent of Locurnia's two moons no longer hung full in the sky. Their spirits might have been lighter. At least the little red moon did not cycle the sky. Some months off, the great silver orb had yet to give away its dominion to the smaller red satellite that heralded in the winter. Such blood-tinged illumination would have turned their collective courage on its head.

They were a party of eight, four of Meran's companions, a healer, and two militiamen. It was all that the justiciar would allow for what the official also considered a most unlikely destination for Ellom to have taken. But Lord Marshal Durans had, if grudgingly, bowed to Meran's pleas, and by default the justiciar bent.

So long as Meran remained in company with the search party, the lord marshal had allowed him the freedom to prove the veracity of his vision. Meran suspected his father did not believe him, but with what Meran had seen in the river, he knew he could turn that assumption.

"Just you wait and see if he's not right," Jon waggled a finger at the soldier.

"You are very forthright in your opinion," the other soldier said with a tone that rang with disapproval before his grumbling companion could respond. He gave Jon a hard, considering stare. "You are that scoundrel, aren't you? The stone carver who has so upset the *Summus Sanctus*."

"And if I am?" Meran heard the challenge in his friend's voice, though his expression remained amicable.

How he effected it, Meran did not know. His own anger beginning to simmer. Yet his dissatisfaction remained unvoiced as Ormand replied, bringing up the rear. "That does not make him wrong. In fact, one copta says he isn't." Ormand tossed said coin in the air which flashed in the moonlight.

The soldier did not look best pleased with what looked like a young man's levity in a grim situation, but his fellow soldier appearing reticent to turn down free coin said, "You're on."

Relief swelled Meran's chest that at least two of the party had faith in him. Of course, Jon had been there when he had roused from the vision. He had witnessed Meran's panic, and the declaration that should they not hurry, Ellom was likely to be dead.

The additional support from Ormand came as a boon. It was something he had not expected.

For long minutes, the party followed Meran over the dark winding trail. He passed many a cave-turned-crypt, their facades, for all intents and purposes, the same, but in his vision, he had beheld one with a difference. The one he sought had natural hollows and protrusions forming a primitive semblance of a face. He just had to find it.

He held his flaming torch aloft and surged forward with an unfaltering resolve. If he must examine them all, he would, and be damned to what anyone else thought of him.

There it was.

Dark-veined creepers surrounding a huge white limestone boulder, cast in ghoulish shadows, complete with its lumpy visage. "This is it," he announced. The party gathered close. Casting a searching gaze over the entrance, Jon crouched to run his hand along the limestone's lower edge and the original dirt runner used to roll it into place.

Meran's nerves ratcheted up a notch. The boulder in question looked untouched. He set his fingers to its top edge, hoping beyond hope to feel a gap—maybe even the touch of cool air escaping from within. To his dismay, he felt nothing.

Could he have been wrong? What if it had not been a vision at all, but a dream influenced by desperation?

No. Meran refused to believe it.

The grumbler huffed, announcing with an officious, self-congratulatory tone. "Shut up tighter than a spinster's cunnie. You there, I can feel the weight of your coin in my pocket already." The soldier leered at Ormand.

"Then you'll be much mistaken," Jon said. "Look here."

Jon pointed at a spot near his feet and, following the direction, Meran spied black-churned dirt beneath a partially broken branch. "Someone's jimmied the stone loose."

The other soldier bent closer to inspect it himself. "Aye. Looks like they managed to lever it open, but the branch has failed, and the stone has rolled near back into place."

"Ellom. We're coming," Meran shouted trying to pull the rock aside with his bare hands. "Well?" He turned back to the stunned soldiers. "Don't stand there like a bunch of pampered priests. Help me."

"Surely you can't think he has gone inside?" the second soldier asked.

"Of course I do," Meran answered, his patience at an end. "Now for the love of the gods, lend me your strength."

Even if they did not believe, they shook free the paralysis of their surprise and all converged to lend a hand. Grunts and groans ensued as arms strained and feet skidded on the slippery dirt, but slowly the heavy rock ground back along its old groove.

"Ellom!" Meran pushed himself through the slim gap they opened, the others attempting to secure the uncooperative boulder. "Ellom we're he—

The stale air hit Meran full force, chill fingers rolling over his skin and through his clothes, making him shiver. But the sight before him brought him up short. The interior revealed beneath the beam of his torch proved nothing like what he expected.

Though dank and dark, the cave walls had been fashioned into intricately carved ledges. At the centre, two sepulchres covered in cut marble rested on the granite tile overlaid on the ground to create a cold floor.

For a moment, Meran did not know where he was, the discrepancy so acute he feared he had brought everyone to the wrong place. He half expected to see Ellom sprawled across a rocky protrusion in the midst of a close, musty, and stark cavern.

He had not expected this.

Ormand broke the spell, pushing past him. He raced after, the beam of his light falling on what looked like a dirty bundle of rags on the floor.

Meran dropped to his knees. "El?" he whispered, hands lifting the young man's head onto his lap. He smoothed his fingers through grit-stained hair and stared into sunken, glazed grey eyes, to see no sign of recognition resting there.

"What is wrong with him?" he demanded as the healer approached.

With all haste, the healer examined the prone young man. "He is beyond parched. If he has been entombed these last four days with not a drop of water, he is in grave danger."

"Heal him," Meran demanded.

"Not here," the man refused. "It requires a working too intricate and demanding." The man took a sharp blade and dragged it across his palm. Holding it above Ellom's face, the healer let the blood drip between those parched lips. "This will tide him over until we can find somewhere more conducive. Now," he held out a leather water-pouch to Meran, "drizzle this into his mouth. Be careful. Not too much or he might be sick. Yes, like that."

Meran did as told, dribbling the liquid over Ellom's wizened and sunken lips. He noted the cool, deathlike feel of Ellom's paper-dry skin. The man's cheeks were hollow and his glassy gaze unresponsive. "Come on, take a little." Even at the trickle of water, Meran saw no response. Panic bubbled deep in his belly. "Please El. Just a little. *Please.*"

Too horrified by his friend's condition, Meran put aside all his questions. They needed to get Ellom to safety, to have the physician attend him, and only then would he demand to know what his friend had been thinking, coming to such a benighted place. Without Meran's vision, there would have been no chance the lad could have walked away from this folly.

Meran stayed by Ellom's side, trying to hide both his fury and his fear, and offering the most minuscule sips of water, even if all it did was moisten the man's throat and tongue. The others hurriedly fashioned a litter from some of the healer's provisions.

Bennan and Ormand took head and tail respectively and carried the man out, the healer calling from behind, "Head to the nearest dwelling, I have need of proper light for a full examination and a place that he may safely stay while he sleeps off the effects of the healing."

Meran made to follow when Jon waved him over, his face sombre. Jon pointed to the verge of the entrance at their feet. Scoured in the dirt were deep runnels, as of a creature scrabbling in a frenzy, trying to dig his way out. Meran's stomach dropped at the thought of his friend in such a panic.

"I don't know why he came," Jon said. "But it was never his intention to stay."

"Poor bastard." The grumbler joined them. "Probably thought he'd die here, and if not for you…" The man trailed off, luminous eyes wide and anxious, his throat bobbing, swallowing hard at the implication.

"Not so cocksure now, are we?" Jon derided as he held out his hand. "A coin, my fine fellow." At the militiaman's look of consternation, he finished, "Your bet is lost."

As if surprised it would be called in, considering the circumstances, the soldier reached into the small purse at his belt and gracelessly handed it over, grumbling all the while.

"And you?" Jon encouraged the other soldier as he moved to his companion's side.

Glowering, the man assumed an air of piety. "I played no part in such gambling, and neither should my foolish friend here. It is against the teachings of the *Summus Sanctus*." He shook his head in distaste. "How is he even to know the other lad's winnings will reach his hands?" Sneering, the soldier grabbed his fellow lawman by the arm, "Come along. Our assistance is needed no longer. Let us return to the justiciar to give our report."

Meran watched the pair hurry out. The grumbler, despite his fellow's insolence, gave Meran a timorous dip of the head and an obsequious, "Sir," as he was hustled out.

Jon snorted. "Perhaps I should have demanded an apology from the pompous arse instead."

"Or perhaps you should not have antagonised him," Meran answered, shaking his head. He did not like the soldier's inference. There had always been the assumption that wealth came with righteousness, and to be poor meant you had somehow fallen short. But Jon's situation was down to Meran, through no fault of his own.

"Anyway," Jon clapped Meran on the back. "I think they believe you now. Once this gets out, everyone will. Respect is what you have earned this day, my good fellow. All you have to do now is watch the money flow in."

Meran held back a laugh. "That is not very likely. If my own father barely believed me, I doubt one such incident will impress anyone else. And those two? One will expound my virtues while deep in his cups and the other, well, he'll behave as if it did not happen at all because it did not come from his precious temple." Besides, wider knowledge of his visions would mean Meran would have to risk the dreamland again. He would have to see if he could reach the prophet by his own determination, and who knew how easy that would be. A successful outcome could not be taken for granted. "All I can say is that it is a pity I did not see in the dreamlands if Ellom will pull through this harrowing experience." His stomach dropped, chill shivers racing his back. "I fear for him."

"Then best we be on our way to get the healer all that he requires." Jon placed a comforting hand on Meran's shoulder. "I for one will not mourn to leave this chill place."

It took the pair only a few moments to catch up to the others, and all continued the journey in tense silence.

By the time they spied a light in the distance, agitation simmered beneath every expression. Ormand and Bennan's arms shook with the strain of carrying Ellom's weight, but neither of them complained as they hurried to reach the little hovel that sheltered beneath the shadow of Silentes Mount. A caretaker's residence, Meran assumed.

Knocking urgently at the heavy wooden door, Meran called through the wood, "Master, make haste, sir. We have a man in need."

Light flooded the stoop as a small, portly man threw the door wide. A receding hairline and tufts of white hair signified his greater age, his face smooth but rosy from the warmth of the fire Meran could see over his shoulder.

"Young sir, what is amiss?"

Displacing Meran, the healer pushed his way forward. The elderly man's eyes widened at the physician's austere appearance, and he allowed the group to surge in before a full explanation could be elicited.

The woman of the house took one look and bustled towards an internal door. "This way, this way, Master," she said, waving the lads carrying Ellom through. The healer strode after and as soon as his patient lay on the bed, Ormand and Bennan were ejected, the door closing behind them with a bang.

Dread silence settled over the room. None seemed to know what to do with themselves.

"Have a seat." The master of the house gestured to a solid wood table, a long-form bench down each side and two carved chairs at top and tail. "Meg, get the young fellows a drink while they await the health of their friend."

The mistress placed a collection of battered tankards on the table and a jug of what smelled suspiciously like ale. Jon in the lead slid along the bench, making room for the others to follow, and helped himself with an encompassing word of thanks to the lady.

"We have sufficient beef broth should you be hungry," she offered. Thick mitt in hand, she brought the pot to the table and then gathered a selection of bowls and utensils and a basket of flatbreads, ignoring any objections they might have had. "Eat up. Lads of your years are always in need of sustenance, and the lot of you are looking more than a little peaked. Let the fire warm you, the ale lighten your spirits, and the food fill your bellies."

Though the broth smelled tempting, Meran felt his nerves too unsettled to contemplate eating anything. There were so many unanswered questions, and worry for his friend dug deep, tormenting his mind as well as his belly. The wait ahead would be torture. Already he fidgeted in his seat, the urge to regain his feet and pace itching the length of his spine.

He did not, however, begrudge either Ormand or Bennan digging in. Carrying Ellom that distance had no doubt made them hungry.

The first sip of ale had Jon screw up his nose, but finding little else to do, the rest supped determinedly. From their looks, the mistress had watered the brew.

Meran gazed around the cosy room. What with the fire roaring on the small hearth, the walls swathed in thick tapestries, and the hardpacked dirt floor covered in woven rugs, it proved itself more than the hovel it appeared from the exterior.

With her duties as host completed, the mistress sank into an exquisitely carved rocking chair. A basket of fabric scraps to her side, she set about knotting the strips together, her hands quick and industrious as she formed the core of a new rag mat. No doubt she was the source of all the cottage's wholesome furnishings.

Neither master nor mistress endeavoured to entertain their unexpected guests, nor satisfy their own curiosity, leaving the lads to their anxious thoughts. The silence grew heavy until Bennan broke it with an impatient sigh. "What takes him so long?"

Meran shrugged. They all knew there were inherent dangers is such healings. Healing magic was singular to each *Voce*, being an ability that filled and enlivened them.

The magic recognised every fibre, every cell of its host, and for most *Voce*, it recognised no other. Only a few were gifted enough to offer their magic to someone else, and that through a gruesome infusion of power and blood. It came with its own perils for both patient and physician.

Meran did not wish to think on it. His agitation grew in leaps and bounds.

"More, I want to know why he was there," Jon said on a low grumble, as if to hide his words from their hosts.

The pair left them to their conversation, the master drawing on his pipe and reading by the wealth of candlelight. They did not lack for candles, the room fair ablaze.

"What possessed him to go to the tombs?" Jon continued. "And what further foolishness made him venture inside?"

"He cannot have been thinking straight," Meran said. "Perhaps he thought himself turned down for the place with Master Romaine and wished to avoid the humiliation. After all, he did not return home after that engagement."

No, but he had shown up at the lord marshal's estate. For a moment, Meran wondered why he was not angrier. But then, Ellom's betrayal had resulted from concern, not from gloating as had Paavo Perico's. Still, they had been long-time friends. Ellom should have come to the gathering if he had been so alarmed.

"You think disappointment drove him to it? Foolishness, indeed." Ormand pushed his plate away and took a sip from his cup. He too made a face, and Meran decided to leave the ale be.

"He seemed excited enough when I saw him at that damned Gratian's villa," Bennan said.

All eyes turned to him, as wide and surprised as Meran's. "He was there?"

"For a moment or two," Bennan replied, his gaze fixed on Meran, and in the depth of those eyes, Meran saw the dawning of accusation. "You were off with the master and his entourage. I went to get Ellom a wine, but the next I saw him he was stalking off, in no mood to talk. I thought you and he must've had words not to his liking."

"I-I never saw him." But Meran's stomach dropped as he remembered the flash of grey eyes in a pale face rife with hurt and humiliation. In his state, he had thought himself hallucinating. Had he been lying to himself? *Gods truth!* Of course, he had. He would recognize the man anywhere, his earnest face dearer to him than ever after what he had offered those few days ago. And yet Meran had not wanted to stop, had not wanted Rune's mastery nor the beauty of what was happening to him to end. He had been selfish and cruel, and as it should, guilt stabbed at him.

"But why come to Silentes Mount?" Jon asked, tone pulsing with exasperation. "Why open a tomb and enter?"

All looked as nonplussed as Meran felt. If Ellom had sought time alone there were many and varied refuges within the city. Places that could easily shelter him from the farsight. Places that could have offered him either solitude or distraction. A tavern, a whorehouse, the university library, one of the dorms... It made no sense that he would come to a place so isolated and so desolate.

The sound of tramping echoed from the yard beyond, a distracting beat calling his attention. A furious rattle shook the door. Startled, the master jumped to his feet, barely opening it ere he was pushed aside to allow entrance to a score of armed and uniformed men.

"What is this?" Meran demanded.

The small room, suddenly overcrowded and seething with tension, had everyone on their feet. More militiamen? But from their looks, none came at the behest of the lord marshal. Meran stared again into the smirking eyes of the pious soldier, now returned with his fellows.

Stepping to the head of the phalanx, a man said in a ringing tenor, "We have reason to believe you are in the company of one Jon Reko." Upon his cloak, the soldier bore the pin of his office. A captain. He waved a rolled scroll in the direction of those clustered about the table. "We bare a warrant of detention."

Meran's gaze flew to where Jon stood, pale but surprisingly composed. Meran's eyes bugged, lax with utter astonishment, as were every one of his friends. Jon ignored them, his attention trained on the uncompromising lawman.

The captain stiffened beneath Jon's nonchalance. "You will not resist," he declared, and as one, the soldiers stepped forward.

CHAPTER FIFTEEN

"You think to arrest him?" Meran demanded, holding up his hand to halt the men and giving the officious subordinate an accusing glare. Had the militiaman returned to the justiciar with a mouthful of lies, all because Jon had taunted him? "On what grounds?"

"A debt that remains unsettled," the captain replied. "It has been brought to the attention of the justiciar. The quarry master demands payment or the return of said purchase."

Jon let out a rude noise. "Said purchase is now a masterpiece called *Indulgence*, as he very well knows, and its value a hundred times the worth of the material that was sold to me."

"That's as it may be." The captain shrugged indifferently. "But the credit terms have been called in and they have not been settled. As you are clearly an itinerant and a reprobate, the justiciar has deemed it best you be brought into custody ere the case is aired."

At the captain's indication, the other soldiers again surged forward.

"By all the hells!" Meran declared. "Step away. I will stand assurance for him. I am Meran Durante. Leave him to my recognizance." Even though he was forbidden to house Jon at his father's estate, maybe he could talk Ormand into sharing with Jon in the servants quarters. And even though he had no money to pay a bond, he could surely get it, if not from his father, then perhaps from Patrice. There had to be something he could do.

Though he tried hard to press through the throng of men to free Jon, the young man was surrounded and none-too-gently brought to heel, though he offered little resistance.

All joined the melee and Meran found himself ignored. Shouts of protest echoed through the room from himself and his companions and they pulled and pushed the soldiers, trying to free their friend.

"You will desist," the captain ordered with an outthrust arm, catching Meran across the cheek. Meran fell back against the table, sending dishes flying and the furniture skidding across the floor with a resonating protest. The mistress shrieked, hands clasping her cheeks, and the master blustered as he found himself knocked to the floor.

"What is the meaning of this?" a deep and commanding voice reverberated across the space. Each participant halted mid-tug, thump, kick and push. "There is a man here, bare moments from his deathbed and I find all here in turmoil! How is a healer supposed to think amidst such ruckus let alone perform his duty to the best of his ability?"

The captain turned from glowering at Meran, and instead confronted the austere gentleman with a baleful grimace. Pulling himself free of Meran's hold, he made his way to Jon, binding the sculptor's hands in front of him. "I want no trouble," he said. "I do nought but what is my duty, sir. I will now take this miscreant to the gaol to await the justiciar's pleasure. Good day to you all."

The soldiers retreated pushing Jon along and leaving all in dumbfounded silence. Though he knew something must be done, Meran had no idea what. This was all on his head. If only he had not defied his father, if only had not shirked his studies; had not made a fool of himself with a bunch of libertines. It was his fault Jon had not secured a patron. If his father had not reneged or Jon not declined Gratian's offer, his debt would be paid and he not be in such a dire strait.

Obligation tore at Meran. He must fix Jon's situation, but how could he leave Ellom when the young man's fate lay in the balance? He had determined that, unlike his father, he would cast none aside— but to choose?

A hand landed on his shoulder, "This is not on you," Ormand said, as if he could read Meran's mind. "I will find aid. Jon will not be abandoned, that I promise. Stay. Ellom will need you when he awakens."

Ormand did not wait for Meran's response, but took off, determination writ large on his face.

Would the young man go to his master to beg assistance? Surely, that would be futile. Once his mind was made up, Durans Durante seldom changed it. Consumed with anxiety, Meran found himself pacing the length of the floor between the outer door and the now-closed bedroom in which Ellom lay. Shaking herself from her shocked amazement, the mistress hurried to her husband, helping him to his feet and fussing over him as he returned to his chair.

He brushed himself off and with a shake of his head, insisted, "I am well, my girl, I am well. 'Tis nought but a few bumps and bruises that will heal easily. Don't fuss." He patted her hand in reassurance and settled himself.

She did not look appeased. "What does the world come to when one is not safe from invasion in one's own home?" Sighing, she returned to her chair.

The remainder of Meran's friends followed suit, a silent accompaniment to his own tumultuous vigil.

Their soft breaths filled the air. The squeak of the mistress' rocker and the flicking of pages the only marks of the passing of time. Step after futile step, Meran strained to hear anything from beyond the bedchamber's closed door. Low murmurs muffled by the wood were the only things to alleviate the tension building within him. Small signs the healer continued to work his magic. Surely, there was still hope.

Meran's heart leapt at the sound of advancing footsteps and he came to a halt, his attention affixed to the door of the bedchamber. It creaked open. The healer emerged again, his shoulders now sagging beneath a patina of exhaustion, his face pale and drawn with dark circles radiating out from beneath his eyes.

"Oh, my stars!" the mistress exclaimed and bustled to get him a plate. She filled the bowl with the thick broth, breaking chunks of the crusty roll into it and shooed Bennan along on his seat to make room for the weary man.

The healer sat, all eyes following him but too anxious to ask the question on their minds. Their concern beating as loud as in Meran's own heart, they all watched the healer down half the fare before he gathered himself and, fastidiously wiping his lips, said, "Your friend has revived."

Relief flooded Meran like a spring tide, though it rankled the man's silence had held them in thrall for so long. A chorus of gratitude burst across the strained silence, the small room erupting into celebration as the two lads almost as one lifted their tankards and clashed them together.

The healer shushed them. "Presently, he sleeps the healing sleep and will do so for many an hour. The infusion required to drag him from death's door, I fear, was of necessity much the stronger than is wont of a single healer, but I have done my best."

And as if to prove his veracity, the healer soon took his leave. "I shall send another of my guild in a few hours to check upon the lad, but for now he needs rest. I ask only that you be wary should he awaken before the healer arrives. A healing of this type is not accompanied by the feelings of repletion as is self-healing. He may be disorientated, confused, even distraught, his emotions in turmoil. Keep him in peace and quiet to eliminate as much distress as possible."

With the physician gone, the master and mistress produced blankets and an abundance of cushions for the lads' comfort. Meran begged off, his worry and guilt prodding at him to sit by his friend's side. No one objected, even if Bennan offered him a sour stare. For the first time, Meran wondered if the lad held some interest in Ellom. But he shook the idea off. Even if it were true, the interest did not appear to be reciprocated.

With dawn beginning to break, Meran found himself still awaiting the new healer's arrival. Only the health now radiating from Ellom's face and body stopped Meran from sending one of his sleeping companions to drag the recalcitrant physician from his bed.

He cast Ellom another look. Fondly, Meran brushed a lock of rich cream hair from the man's forehead, tempted to follow with a caress to Ellom's flushed cheek. If only the young man would awaken. Above all, Meran longed for the reassurance of Ellom's recognition.

Beneath the lids, Ellom's eyes fluttered back and forth, dreaming. It would not be long.

Ellom stirred. A deep sigh and the reflexive tightening of Ellom's grip around Meran's hand evidenced his friend was coming to. Meran's heart beat faster in anticipation, eager and yet wary of his friend's reaction.

The thick veil of Ellom's lashes fluttered and his eyes opened, the huge dark pupils shrinking to pinpricks as they adjusted to the dim morning light. Meran held Ellom tighter as he startled at the unfamiliarity of his location and the horrific memories that would no doubt follow him into the day.

"You are found," Meran whispered with heartfelt reassurance. "You are well."

Ellom stared around with huge eyes until they landed on Meran's face and took his presence in with a feverish, desperate intensity. "You found me?"

Despite how well he looked, Ellom's voice came thick with disuse, or perhaps it was raw from screaming for help. The realisation rocked, a new wave of emotion pounding over Meran.

Leaning forward, he palmed Ellom's jaw, his hold soothing but firm. Keeping his voice low and intimate, he confirmed, "I found you."

Ellom's eyes shone with tears. "How? I-I… was en-entombed. By the gods! No one could have…" But the young man could not finish as the horror of his experience returned. A fit of weeping overpowered him, tugging at Meran's heart, and he rose from his seat. Gripping Ellom in a tight embrace, he crooned nonsense and dropped kisses on the top of his friend's hair.

"You are safe. You are found. I found you. I have you. We none could rest until we had you back."

For a while, his words had little effect, the sounds growing harsher and more ragged. Meran silently cursed the absent healer. There should be some potion or other that would offer Ellom some respite. Instead, Meran held him and hoped it would be sufficient.

An abrupt shift came over Ellom, a stiffening of his body in Meran's embrace and the next Meran knew, he was pushed back hard, Ellom's words hissing with fury, "How could you?"

Confusion surged, the dire thought striking that Ellom had not wanted to be rescued. Horror echoed through Meran until Ellom's further words sank in.

"It was *I* that opened your eyes." Ellom's features contorted with rage, and yet grief danced in his eyes. "*I* that offered you relief and freedom from your torment. Did I then deserve to be so spurned as if what I had given you was nothing?"

The accusation almost struck Meran dumb. Remembering the physician's warning, he tried to overlook Ellom's tumultuous emotion. "El, please. I am sore sorry." He grabbed for the prone man's flailing hands, holding them steady, kissing the knuckles, trying desperately to placate him. "You know that was not the way of it."

"I know what I awoke within you, what I alone first intuited," Ellom said. "It gave you peace and yet you act as if coming from me it is no longer good enough."

"No, no." Meran denied, but the truth behind Ellom's words niggled. If Gratian had not made a fool of him, Meran was sure he would have gone to the merchant master in the hopes of more. "For the love of the gods, El. We have been friends forever, why would I do that to you?"

"I don't know." Ellom flopped back onto the pillows and shut his eyes, his brow furrowed and lips twisted as if he chewed on his response and found it distasteful. "You chose to go with Jon full knowing that I could offer you what they did. I, one of your best friends. And yet you turned your back on me."

"I did," Meran confessed. It was exactly what he had done, but he'd had his reasons. Not that in the light of what happened, they seemed of import anymore. "It was thoughtless and for that, I humble myself. I beg your forgiveness. But, we are such friends that I would never spurn you. El, I mastered my calling, for you."

"Pray, what?" Shock registered in the stormy grey eyes, heat suffusing Ellom's pale cheeks.

Meran gathered Ellom's hands in his. "I passed the one vision. You had to be found, or you would have died."

Ellom's mouth opened as if to refute the supposition, but his lips quivered as the tempest in his gaze resolved into shimmers of unshed tears.

"Why did you do it?" Meran encouraged softly. "Why did you go to Silentes Mount?"

"I-I didn't mean for it to happen, I swear." Tears thickened Ellom's voice.

"Then why do such a foolish thing?"

Ellom took a shuddering breath, contrition shadowing his features as he swallowed. "I wasn't. I-I... It hurt, Meran, to see how you were with them. I felt pierced through and through, so much so that I wanted you to suffer beneath that same pain. I thought only to hide where none would find me—"

"So that I would feel your loss," Meran concluded.

Ellom nodded, the tears falling silently down his cheeks. "I intended only to spend the one night sheltered between the graves. There is enough stone on Silentes Mount to hinder the farsight. Why I thought to enter my family's mausoleum, I don't know... the autumn winds were cold, I guess, but the branch broke and trapped me inside." Ellom's mouth opened and closed as if he would say more, but the memories stole his voice.

Pity flooded Meran at Ellom's distress. He squeezed Ellom's suddenly cold hands, noting the once dirty, bloodied, and abraded nails were again pristine.

No one deserved what had happened to Ellom, be they the most foolish and self-destructive person in all of Locurnia. Ellom had suffered the consequences of his immaturity and selfishness. "I forgive you," he said.

"I don't know how?" Ellom whispered. "When all I wished to do was crush you."

"You don't mean that." Yet the guilt paling the man's cheeks to a white parchment spoke otherwise.

"I did." Ellom's chin rose with what defiance he could muster. "I wanted to hurt you so badly; for you to feel the pain of rejection that stabbed me at the sight of you with them... with him. I saw how you submitted to that man, how you revelled in it and knew that I could never compare."

"El, please. I did not do it to spite you, that I promise. The vision, it... I just hoped for some relief."

"Do you think that I would not have given it to you? But now I find myself supplanted by another you deem my superior."

There it was; the obsession that he feared would overwhelm their friendship. But it was too late to turn back the dial on what they had done, so Meran had to find a way to forge through a dilemma he had wrought. He had a choice to make. To lose a dear friend, or accept the foibles of them both and turn it to their advantage.

"That is not true," he defended resting a hip against the bed's edge and sinking closer. "You did open my eyes to something that I had not known about myself, the deepest of desires that I fear is addictive."

He still yearned to be dominated, to be ordered and commanded and mastered and praised. It had aroused him more than any other act of passion ever had. It painted him weak and craven in his own eyes, yet he still wanted more. "But I know I cannot let it run roughshod over me. I am a lord marshal's son, a Durante, and it is too dangerous to share such a weakness. It can only be exploited; unless you help me."

"Help you?" Ellom's confusion turned to a glimmering hope.

"Aye," Meran said, his lips twitching with a reticent smile, a welling of shyness bubbling upward. He would not succumb to just anyone, only the one who could be trusted with such an intimate desire. "I am not alone in learning lessons over these last days, I think."

"Pray, what?"

Meran squirmed, unready for a full confession. "I will tell you later, but suffice to say, I wish you alone to command me when the need comes upon me. Will you consider it?"

Silence followed.

The pull, when it came, took Meran by surprise. He found himself mashed against Ellom's chest, the man's arms like a prohibitive vice, no trace of Ellom's debilitation left.

Eye to eye, Meran looked into an earnest grey maelstrom, their breaths mingling like the winds swirling in a dervish between them, the tips of their noses touching. That his first instinct was not to draw away hardly came as a surprise. The power behind Ellom's determination tantalisingly captured his imagination.

Yet he needed to make one thing clear from the outset. He still had something he needed to do before he could put the past behind him. He had a man to face and his own self-esteem to redeem, and, most importantly, a pledge to accept on Jon's behalf even though the artist had foolishly refused it.

"If we are to continue with this, there is one thing that I will not abide," he whispered above Ellom's alluring firm lips.

"And that is?"

"You will swear to keep your discontent in check, for I will not swear fidelity, except in this one regard. Can you do that?"

In solemn silence, Ellom considered, and Meran held his breath wondering if his tentative offer was sufficient to heal the rift between them, to maintain their friendship as it morphed into this new and viable form. He watched as his friend's grimace slowly turn to a feral smile that could only mean assent.

Meran allowed Ellom's elegant fingers to traverse the contours of his back to the nape of his neck and apply a much-anticipated pressure. He found his lips consumed by a feverish, undeniable kiss that set his body to trembling. His longing had been answered. He had seen this potential in Rune Gratian, but like this, Ellom looked just as wonderful, enticing, and powerful.

The incident at the villa had been a consummation of betrayal, but this was an expression of a deep and abiding yearning, a craving on both their parts.

Ellom broke the kiss first. "We are fools, both." He smiled. "And I solemnly swear that never again will I let my pique get the better of me. When the son of Lord Marshal Durans Durante is at play, then I will not interfere, but when it is only myself and Meran, I promise with all my heart to sate every one of his needs for submission."

"And for that, you have my heartfelt thanks." Meran smiled, itching now to hear Ellom's strong and sure authority. That depth of voice that resonated within and made Meran shake beneath the intensity of the feelings it induced. "Now, will you please command me?"

"Of course. How could I not with such sweet begging?" Ellom replied, his grey eyes sparkling. "And as proof, I will now demand your silence."

With that, Ellom flipped them with greater ease than Meran had expected. Ellom's lips were like a ravishing flood, washing over and through Meran. He let himself drown in the ensuing sensations, all while luxuriating in the necessity to stifle every sound of the bliss burgeoning deep within him.

CHAPTER SIXTEEN

All the anxiety that twisted and tightened in his chest as Meran contemplated the coming confrontation dissipated into despondency at the hollow echo of his knocking.

That a guard no longer stood at Rune Gratian's gate should have been Meran's first hint. The second, the hushed solitude that stifled each step he took across grounds that led to buildings, solemn and forlorn in their abandonment.

Still disbelieving his intuition, Meran listened for a response from within, breath bated. He heard nothing.

Sighing, he made to retreat, glad that he had not brought Ormand for support. The man was about Durante business at the docks. Later, he would join them at the Petrel's End in time to meet Jon, newly returned from his incarceration.

Now, it appeared, his opportunity to demand justice for Rune and Paavo's despicable behaviour was lost due to ill-timing. The few days he had awaited to gather his courage had been three too many. His face heated, not from anger, but a burgeoning disappointment, the cause of which he refused to examine too closely.

A clack of handle and squeal of hinge made him stop, his heart giving one solid thud as the smooth polished door cracked open. Maico's familiar face peered out.

"Young Master Ormand?" Incredulity stretched across the man's features as the servant swung the door wide. "It is good to see you so hale and hearty. You were somewhat worse for wear when last we parted."

"Ah?" Confusion teased his brows. When Meran had last been at the villa, he had seen no sign of the servants—not once the festivities had begun in earnest.

"You do not remember?" The man did not seem surprised. "The master had me take you to the halls, to your rooms. He feared to let you make your own way."

Gratian had ensured he had made it home safely? Well, this was news. Perhaps he was not such an arse, after all. Yet, he had still done what he had done, and Meran's humiliation still demanded validation. Meran firmed his resolve. This knowledge would not make him revisit his motivations—nothing but the recognition of the man's errant ways and a full apology would suffice.

"Is Rune in residence?" he asked, but already his heart sank as he flipped a glance over the servant's shoulder. The furnishings and statuary within view were covered in swaths of fabric.

"I am sore sorry," Maico answered, his expression rife with curiosity. "He is not. My master has returned to his estate on the Summer Isles, ere the crossing become too fraught with the coming winter sea."

"Oh." His tension crashed at the announcement, leaving him consumed with a roiling purposelessness in the pit of his stomach. "I'm equally sorry to have missed him." There would be no chance at reconciliation now, not that he wanted that. No expression of regret would ever be enough to alleviate the hurt that needled him inside.

As he started to turn away, Maico interrupted his retreat with a gentle touch to the arm of his coat.

"If you will wait just one moment," he said, and with Meran's attention caught, the servant disappeared back inside, his footsteps ringing in the silence. Fading and then returning quickly, Maico held forth a folded parchment. The servant's interest appeared even more piqued, though he was too professional to seek its satiation. "Master Gratian anticipated that you might come. He left me specific instruction to pass this to you. If you wish, you may take a moment in the garden to read it."

"Thank you," Meran said, reaching tentatively for the missive, his fingers numb as he gripped it tight. Meran retreated to the now slumbering courtyard, hearing the door close with a soft *snick* behind him. He struggled against the hope that threatened to displace his plummet into melancholy. He could not read too much into the situation. Rune Gratian was gone, after all.

Alone, Meran sat in the lush cloister, its fountain as mute and as lifeless as the dwelling behind him. In the midmorning light, the beauty of it still echoed with the sense of peace and the last blush of growth before winter's sleep took it. A place Jon would love to paint. But there would be no chance to argue Jon's cause now, Meran mourned.

He sat for a moment, commanding his breath into a calm rhythm, and turned his attention to the sealed parchment. Letters forming the name Ormand were drawn across the outside, even though Gratian knew it to be a misnomer. Perhaps he thought to save Meran the indignation of further gossip. But the man had known he would come. The message proved it.

With trembling fingers, Meran broke the seal and unfolded the parchment, noting the graceful lettering, the bold curves and extravagant flourishes. The hope that Gratian had taken the time to pen it himself niggled at Meran. He wanted no other to know the words Rune had meant for him alone, he longed for that small intimacy. Now, he would never know.

Blinking, he opened his eyes to refocus on the fine script, letting out one last fearful breath as he gathered his courage.

Master Meran,

It is good should this note find you well.

Word of your heroic deeds have been on every lip these last days and I fear none can miss how your reputation as a seer will grow exponentially. Your sire must be well satisfied.

For myself, I find I am at a loss for how to proceed, but only that I must beg forgiveness. The man I once knew and admired is that man no longer, but has become avaricious and arrogant, thoughtless and cruel. It will not surprise you, but some men are become as hungry for wealth as dragons are for hoard. I had not wished to become such a one.

Yet, to my consternation, I find Paavo Perico has sunk to such levels of petty vengeances—of which I unwittingly found I had played a part in regard to you— that I can no longer countenance further association with him.

Needless to say, any and all covenants with the pirate have become void in the wake of my enlightenment.

However, I will not bandy more words, nor make any further excuse. I have wronged you. Whether intentional or not does not matter. I am compelled by decency to offer you my apologies. I fear, not alone did my actions cause you grief on the night of the celebration: but that my further offer of patronage to Jon Reko was seen as extravagant and as an affront and not an expression of the depths of my sorrow nor my desire for restitution. This I understand, for now I think on it further, you were no courtesan to be paid for what you offered so freely, and in my own arrogance for absolution, I should never have treated you so.

However, I know the dire strait of your dear friend and still wish to assist him, though my own means have suffered a severe setback. I would hope that the enclosed will not be deemed as offensive for I understand what it is to be penniless and without prospect. I, too, was a waif that rose from the gutter. His work has such freedom, such expression and beauty and decadence, that to squander it would be a crime beneath the both of us. I trust you will do what is right in this regard.

For now, I salute you, Meran Durante, scholar and seer, and though I shall in all likelihood, not return for some time to my estate in Dun, I wish you only your future health, happiness and prosperity.

Your servant,
Rune Gratian, Merchant Master

Meran read the letter more than once, his feelings in turmoil. Every word made him boil with fury. He did not accept the apologies nor the explanations, nor Rune's unequivocal admissions of guilt. He could not abide the emotionless tenor of these words scribed on paper.

He wanted raw, heartfelt anguish at the travesty those men had wrought on his self-worth. He wanted the ability to rage, to blame, to see another bend beneath the weight of their perfidy. He did not care about any of the others, only Rune mattered. He wanted the man's soul bared; the master, the domineer brought to his knees in supplication.

But Gratian's very absence stole the avenue of Meran's expression, as if his validity had been torn loose. As it stood, Gratian's words fell far short to satisfy his indignation.

The parchment shook in his hand, mere minutes from being torn to shreds. But then there was the promissory note for Jon. This was what, he told himself, he had ultimately come here for. He could not rip apart that gilded paper.

Meran could not let his own pique stand in the way of another's wellbeing. A friend whose loyalty had dictated he turn down the original overture's outrageous sum. This amount, not even an eighth of the total Rune had previously named, amounted to that of the standard contribution a patron bequeathed for the commissioning of a worthy piece of statuary, plus a little more. Jon would not be flush, but he would not starve. He would have the wherewithal to pay back his debt, both to the quarry master and to Ormand's father who had unexpectedly discharged the bond. And he could hire a studio for at least the next two years, which would provide a roof over his head while he worked.

Rune had made no stipulations and commissioned no artwork, sculpture or otherwise. He looked to be leaving that up to the artist himself. Graciousness or disinterest? Meran could not decide. From his limited experience, he had seen the man's love of artistry; he was a connoisseur not of indifference but of freedom of expression. Perhaps he knew Jon's temperament and trusted his innate taste, though some touted it as only bad.

Well, Meran determined, Jon would never know the identity of this benefactor. The money would not be given in Gratian's name, nor would it be given in Meran's. But he knew someone who might be persuaded to stand in his stead. Finding himself with the sudden need of a stiff drink, he determined to secure his wanted agreement and then make for the Petrel's End to await his friends.

The low rumble of society echoed through the tavern. Men gathered in clusters around the polished and carved wooden tables and by the huge stone fireplace. Meran sat surrounded by his friends.

While he did not begrudge their desire to salute Jon with an evening of revelry, he had other things on his mind. That was until Ormand made his way to the gathering and sat down beside him at the booth they had claimed for themselves.

"What did you hear?" Meran asked, hand on Ellom's arm, holding his curiosity at bay. Meran leaned towards Ormand, the man's green eyes glittering with excitement.

"He took ship two days ago," Ormand canted his head closer to whisper in Meran's ear. "After there was a rather public to-do outside Gratian's offices. The rumours fly every which way, but I found one who had actually witnessed it. It seems the two have parted ways in less than amicable circumstance. Master Perico disliked to be chided for his bad behaviour in front of the masses and the Gratian fellow accused him of piracy, among other things. Such an accusation was not accepted with good grace, and that it did not come to blows is only down to the fact Gratian's ship was ready to set sail."

The news left Meran ambivalent. Could Gratian not have known of Perico's designs? From his willingness to initiate the carouse, it did not seem likely. Rune Gratian had taken charge, taken control, and Perico had only played second fiddle. But, what if Rune had desired the liaison, desired Meran in his own right?

Meran crushed the errant thought. What did it matter anymore? The man was gone—and for good as far as Meran was concerned. No matter the intention, his trust in the merchant master was forfeit and no amount of wishing could change that.

"Thank you for letting me know." He patted the back of Ormand's hand. Both became distracted by the uproar that suddenly surrounded them, Jon's name echoing on nearly every tongue.

Somewhat subdued, Jon forged his way through the gathered throng and to their table. A thick drape to their back kept out the chill from the series of small leadlight windows placed high along the outer wall. It was an extravagance for such an establishment and an incentive that kept the poorer citizen from its richly carved doors. For the first time ever, Jon looked uncomfortable with his surroundings.

With his mind now somewhat settled by Ormand's news, Meran allowed Jon a moment to relax and for the barkeep to send a jug of ale the artist's way.

"'Tis my shout," Meran called and flipped a coin to the taverner.

Jon raised his brows in thanks, all traces of concern dissipating. Despite his dire financial straits, Jon had still come at Meran's invitation, though he knew he could ill-afford it. Well, Meran had the remedy for that, if Jon would accept.

Meran let Bennan raise a toast to Jon's freedom and Ellom's good health, even though a shadow still remained behind the slate grey of the young man's eyes. No one could suffer as he had and not be changed by it. Meran had heard from Ellom's mother of the nightmares he had and would no doubt have for years to come. All Meran had in his arsenal to hold the man's memories at bay were his friendship and their continued intimacy. It fell far short, he knew, but Ellom had so far refused to speak of it again. Meran hoped he would, in time.

Containing his impatience, Meran let the conversation evolve until Jon had finished his tankard. Excusing himself to Ellom, Meran rose from his seat, indicating for the artist to follow him to a quiet corner near the end of the bar.

Without preamble, he leaned down to Jon's ear. "I have a proposition."

Jon swept his impertinent gaze up from Meran's boots and over his body until their eyes met again.

"You are an arse." Meran laughed, the tension building inside him dissipating at Jon's feigned horror. "Not that kind of proposition."

"Well thank the gods for that small mercy. I would not have liked to offend a friend by turning him down, but, well, I have tackle just as you have tackle… and I prefer other trappings."

Meran laughed again. "How will you know until you try?"

Jon made a strangled noise and, laughing even harder, Meran thumped him on the back as if to stop him choking. It elicited only an exaggerated, "*Ooph.*" It would take more than that to make Jon sway on his feet. A tenacious bastard, at any given moment Jon had the wherewithal to drop Meran on his arse should he choose to do so.

Meran sobered. "Now, will you be serious for but a moment, I have some news of great import for you."

With an elaborate hand gesture, Jon indicated for Meran to proceed.

"Here." Meran pulled a missive from his coat and handed it over.

A wry expression flitted over Jon's features as he took the parchment and broke the seal. The promissory note fluttered free to be caught by the tips of Jon's fingers. He looked at the sum, and at Meran with a furrowed brow.

"I cannot take your money."

"I assure, it is not mine," Meran answered, truthfully. "You know damn well, Father has control of all my funds—"

"*His*, then?"

Meran sighed. He knew who Jon referred to, and it was not his sire. A canny guess, but if the artist had read the previous missive from Gratian that he himself had spurned; the conclusion might not be such a leap in the dark. Curiosity burgeoned into regret that Meran had not taken the opportunity when presented. Neither could he now ask if Jon had done as demanded and burned it or had it still in his possession. Either way, it was lost to his curiosity.

"No, no, no," he lied. "For the pity's sake, read on."

Jon's gaze fell to the letter and the delicate script etching the page. He read quickly, his eyes growing wider. "This is from your sister."

"Aye."

"But how? Why?"

"She has funds of her own, from our mother," he answered. "And unlike me, she is deemed wise enough to have access and the freedom to use it as she wills. Look, see?" he pointed out his sister's stipulations. They were his own, to be honest, but she had agreed to what he wanted and to stand in his stead as patron. "She has a commission for you.

One that is close to both of our hearts. This is what she pays you for."

"A tribute to your brother?"

"Not him alone. A memorial to them all."

"And, it is to be displayed in Central Square? A bequeath from the Durantes to the citizens of Dun?" Jon looked disbelieving. "She does recall that half the populace of Dun would prefer I lost the use of my fingers rather than take up my tools again."

Meran shook his head with vigour. "She trusts you. I trust you."

If he accepted it, Meran knew, Jon would give his whole heart to his cause and do it the justice it deserved. Then all of Dun could share the memory of the one great man amongst many who had fought and died in the jungles of Aleia for the salvation of all *Vocekind*. A worthy man whose humanity spoke of his sense of fun, his vulnerability, and his dedication to both his duty and his people. A man the likes of which Rune Gratian could never be.

This thought alone offered Meran some meagre satisfaction, producing a stark and brittle smile. Meran could not deny his bitterness, his fear of the strength of his folly. That despite everything, his greatest regret was that something more had not eventuated. Lacking in neediness or fickle emotion, Rune had a commanding maturity that drew Meran's attention even to this point. But Meran had no time for rue. He determined to shut down the strange disappointment tweaking his own heart for something that could never be.

No, he had his life, he had his loyal and trustworthy friends, and he had Ellom to scratch his itch. If there was still a spark missing, then Meran could live with that, if only to avoid the danger of making a fool of himself again.

Equally, he now had purpose and the ability to submerse himself in his magic. And he had Philo to lead him on his unavoidable path. All he had now to do was to convince his father his life was on track. With that achieved, he would be set.

He looked at Jon now, fearful the man would still turn him down. The monument not only to his brother's heroism and sacrifice, but his people's, was as necessary as his next breath. "Please say that you will accept it."

Jon took a deep breath, pursing his lips as if undecided. "I will," he said. "And with my thanks, the next shout is mine."

EPILOGUE

"Meran! Wake up."

The call echoed, reminiscent of Ellom's that had shaken him from his sleep and the vision that had hounded him near on a year and a half earlier. But this time it was different. This time he had been awake when the vision had washed over him.

A commotion ensued, a plethora of raised voices only mildly piquing Meran's curiosity. The tumult could not fully penetrate the shimmering cocoon of calm that shrouded him, so different from how the visions normally took him. To this point, they had always followed the course of his first experience with the prophet; apart from the use of hampr, of course. But, this? This was new and intriguing.

"I can't reach him." Ellom's voice rose tight with tension.

He and a group of Meran's friends had been celebrating Meran's return to the apartment at the university halls. His father had finally deemed Meran's behaviour sufficient to allow him a certain amount of freedom again. They had gathered to christen the rooms with a cask of red wine and Jon's required barrel of ale.

Leaning back into the daybed with Ellom curled at his left, he had been in the midst of boisterous conversation. They had discussed Ormand's new position and teased him that he would more likely be mistaken for the cabin boy by this captain than as Durans Durante's newest factor. They had been heckling him unrepentantly about the man's reputation.

"On board a ship, the captain is god," Bennan taunted, "and you'll be nought but his lackey. Who's to know the work he'll put you to?" The man then proceeded to make a lewd gesture. The room erupted with raucous guffaws.

"I am in the employ of the lord marshal to ensure the safety of his precious cargo," Ormand overrode them, his face a bouquet of blushes. "This captain will not make me do his bidding."

"And who is to stop him?"

"Enough, enough," Jon interrupted their knowing laughter, demanding their forbearance. "Enough of your teasing. Let the man rest."

This latter only served to make the man in question blush brighter. Meran went to throw a conciliatory arm over Ormand's shoulder when something hit him.

Like a cascading fall of golden light, a curtain descended and Meran's simulacrum was wrenched from his body, his heart a thundering tattoo of astonishment and his breath rushing free.

He could hear Philo's insistent call like the wail of a banshee while the dismayed chatter of his friends rustled as loudly as the chittering of crickets on a fine day. He looked down to see them clustered close about his form encased in a sheath of light, wariness on every expression.

"What's happening?"

"Meran?"

The body's eyes remained closed, the expression calm and distant.

"By the Lord's hairy ball sac! What is that?"

"Come, lad. Now," the disembodied voice of Philo demanded. Meran felt himself drawn towards the dark veil that always stood between the dreamlands and that of the Plains of Elysia and its wondrous river. "Boy. Take my hand."

Meran could not refuse though the terror and concern of his friends tried to drag him back.

"It's like an emanation of force. I can't breach it."

"No," Philo forbade him, drawing Meran's attention back to the star-studded night. "Time is of the essence. Nothing like this has happened before. You must come. You must read the tides. Make haste, make haste."

Meran acquiesced to Philo's command, leaving those clustered around his light-encapsulated body far behind as he rode the gleaming beam of power. The night swallowed him. Though it made no difference, he found himself holding his breath as he passed through the void. The river's undercurrents wrested him this way and that and threatened to tear him free of Philo's grip.

He held on.

Breaking through the surface, he found the river's course in chaos. Before him, a blue stream of turmoil jetted towards the sky, the water frothing beneath the roiling geyser. "By the gods! What is it?"

"It is a vent, the influence of an imminent event that has the power to alter the river's course in an unprecedented manner," the shade of Philo explained.

For the first time, Meran could see the prophet's spectre and he gaped at Sofie's apt description. The prophet looked as old as a god and as majestic, a brilliant vision of silvery-white.

"It is your calling," the prophet said.

"What must I do?" Meran asked, embarrassed by his own timidity.

Philo threw his arm wide, pointing to the maelstrom, "You must see what cataclysm comes to pass."

Meran knew that Philo expected him to immerse himself in the disruption's flow. Easier said than done. The fountaining flood of churning power rushed like the wind in a gale, the waters falling in a cascade that rumbled like thunder.

He was afraid, and yet exhilarated at the thought of performing a duty that no one but he could accomplish. Being the only seer in five hundred years to have made it through the dreamlands and onto these sacred planes, he had to see it through. Still his trembling appeared to outweigh his courage, and he floundered for a moment.

Fighting down his nerves, Meran shook himself. Taking a fortifying breath, he kicked forward. The fountaining sheet slammed over him, bludgeoning him under, even as he gasped in shock at the reality of its force.

Meran found himself thrust downward by the sheer volume of visions that had surged through the streams, turning and pounding down in an undeniable gush. He found himself pushed to the dark core at the rift's centre.

Like the eye of a storm, he emerged into a void of calm that sucked him in, and he found himself surrounded by gloom. He could see nothing until lines began to form through the darkness. A lattice of shadows and hollows resolved themselves into mud bricks lain atop each other until a circular wall surrounded him, encompassing everything.

Light filtered down on him from above, stabbing at his eyes. Meran hissed and looked away, rolling circles and flashes obscuring his vision. Bowing his head, he gazed down into nothing until the dancing lights petered out into a deep pool of darkness… darkness that moved.

A silhouette formed below; its industrious movements

accompanied by the scrape of metal against stone.

A well.

Though the detail remained indistinct, Meran found himself floating above what looked to be a lad digging at the bottom of a well.

I've found it, an unfamiliar voice declared in a foreign language, and yet somehow in the vision's midst Meran knew it instinctively.

It came to him like sound through deep water and he noted a dark stain beginning to spread across the ground.

As if from a great distance above came the muffled response. *If this… ruse to get… that dirty hole, you… mistaken.*

There followed an altercation. Disembodied voices threw insults at each other until they cut off abruptly.

The form blocking the light from above pulled back and the other figure turned back to his work.

At a loss, Meran could not see how the digging of a well could result in the tumult that assaulted the river's course, and yet this was its centre.

With a determined motion, the figure thrust his spade in and heaved. Meran stared in awe as an object broke free, blue light flaring bright in the darkness. Spots of blue flickered through his mind and Meran found himself confused and blinded by the swirling mists that followed.

As if in answer to his unspoken question, the startled voice boomed from above again, *What is that?*

Ghost light. Meran heard not a voice this time, but the boy's frantic, fear-filled thought.

There ensued a scrabbling. A thud. Meran managed to pull himself together in time to feel the sides of the well encroaching like the imagined, unseen weight of a cavern. A feeling of suffocation took his breath as the new occupant bent and reached out a hand to take the thing that pulsed like a broken heart.

Don't touch it.

Ignoring the command, fingers closed possessively about its girth. The gloom filled with a flare of power so overwhelming, Meran's ears and eyes seemed to burst, and a shriek of disbelief stole his breath. He feared for the integrity of his simulacrum as waves of magical energy washed through him, threatening to tear him apart and send him crashing back into his body.

Then came a herculean command. Foreign, and not from Philo.

"Know me, boy. Come to me."

Meran struggled to find himself as his mind shuddered away from the terror of that order. Rolling like thunder, a humourless laugh billowed over him, pressing him down until its weight crushed his likeness. Squeezed smaller and smaller, he became nothing but a mote of dust to be thrown this way and that. He battered against a stream of bubbles, surging to the surface, and found himself sucked through their fluid skin.

Visions inundated him, panic rushing through every tingling, sparking nerve. Like the visions of Aleia, blood and death walked, but not in the jungles but the vales of Locurnia. Other visions burst in to take their place, distorting his perceptions of the enemy. Faces everywhere. A plethora of grimaces, greed, friendship, welcome, betrayal.

"What is this? What is happening?" Meran cried out in confusion. "What am I to do?"

He did not know who these strangers were or what they might mean to him or his beloved countrymen until he felt himself encompassed in a vivid and present image.

A man with the bearing of a leader. A warrior. An emanation hung about him like a red veil of violence—a killer—yet his aura danced with the colours of a prism, the likes of which Meran had never seen before. A spectacular, intriguing, and enticing specimen.

Tall, broad, and imposing, the warrior's expression brooked no opposition. Meran could feel the command radiating off him like the rays of the summer sun…

His heart fluttered as memories of Rune Gratian sparked, mortification adding to the heat he felt claim his body. He had thought on that man far too often since the humiliating events of those days.

And now, this apparition reeked with similarities, the style of the man's short, dark, sandy-brown hair validating the comparison. The fashion of Velkory, of the Summer Isles or the city of Atena that nestled at the mouth of the Meith River to the north of Locurnia. But like Rune, this man was a *Voce*, magic visibly rippling through him, even if it could only be detected in the vision.

To what did he portend? Meran had no idea. No idea until the warrior reached out his hand, his fingers slipping through the gaps in an arcing swirl of silver fins on the top of a tall metal stand. On a central cup sat a dark blue gem encrusted with a cracked coating of black. It no longer glowed with either wild or ambient light but lay still on its metal bed as the man's large hand closed around it and drew it aloft.

Without knowing how, Meran knew this to be the same gem he had seen freed from the bottom of the well. A treasure like no other. It was the size of an ox heart; rough and raw and beautiful. A talisman of magic, its finding had torn a great rift beneath the River of Time.

But what could Meran do with this information? He could not return to himself and insist he go on a quest to find something when he had no idea where it was. Nor did he know the true import of it, other than that its existence set his heart trembling with trepidation.

"Search the river, boy," the prophet's voice broke through his churning thoughts. "Follow the new currents for I know not this gem nor if my written words have been scattered to the winds. You must keep seeking."

Even as he reached for Philo's comforting presence, the instruction failed to placate Meran. He had no understanding of what to search for.

The spectre's hand gripped him as if he were no longer the mote being tossed by the fates, but himself again. "Find the man," Philo commanded.

The image of the unknown warrior filled Meran's head and made him shiver with both fear and anticipation. Instinct demanded he refuse.

Unperturbed by the strength of Meran's mixed emotions, the prophet repeated, "Find the man. Free the gem. Fix the course of the world."

The mantra, a stark directive, circled around in Meran's head. Meran opened his eyes and found himself returned to his friends. The gathering peered at him, their faces filled with concern and their mouths with questions.

"What happened?" Ellom asked, squirming to fit beneath his arm.

Meran found it both comforting and annoying but still he pulled Ellom close, glad of his reality and warmth.

Ellom nuzzled his nose against Meran's neck. "We couldn't reach you, that thing came—"

"The prophet called me," Meran interrupted. He eyeballed his friends. "He had a message for me. An important one that could not wait for sleep."

They all returned his gaze expectantly, and although he hesitated to tell any in case they thought him deluded, he knew they of all were the most trustworthy. His father still had not lifted most of Meran's restrictions. Meran had made promises to finish his studies with the mysteries department in order to gain the use of his apartment again, limiting his free time. He would need all the help that he could get to clarify the meaning behind the vision. Their expressions, to his relief, conveyed their eagerness.

"What must we do?" Jon asked softly, after Meran had relayed everything that he could remember.

In bemusement, Meran shook his head. "Find the man. Free the gem. Fix the world," he repeated.

"That is easily said, but how will such a feat be accomplished?" The concern that creased Ellom's brow reflected Meran's own apprehension.

What man? What gem? What issue faced the world?

A shrug was all answer Meran could give. "At this point, I don't know, but I assure you, I intend to find out."

Seer Quest: Alliance - Legend of the Ancients

A fledgling seer. A cataclysmic vision. Can he convince the fated warrior to stand between their people and impending doom?

Meran Durante is on a knife's edge. Tormented by the visions of Locurnia burning, and the horrific fate of Patrice, his beloved sister, Meran confronts the one man destined to stop the slaughter. Yet facing the fascinating, but ruthless, Leon Ricci, a perilous attraction sparking between them morphs to dangerous contention, bringing all Meran's plans crashing down.

Fear laces Lord Marshal Leon Ricci's rage. His rising interest for the handsome Durante withers at the youth's blatant attempt to suborn him with knowledge no man should possess. Secrets that would leave his clan, and all he cares for, in jeopardy.

With time running short before Lord Ricci returns to his stronghold, Meran fears he'll be unable to alter the magnetic man's misconceptions before the future's deadly events overwhelm them all.

Can Meran bring the implacable Ricci to heel or will his mistake force Leon to reject taking that first step on the quest destined to save their world?

Seer Quest: Covenant is the action-packed third book in the LGBTQ Legend of the Ancients, Books of Locurnia Fantasy series. If you like epic quests, fantasy laced with high heat romance, and clashing protagonists then you'll love this magic-filled adventure.

Moon Rite: Book One Legend of the Ancients

Two rites stand before him. Fail one and he will be powerless, fail the other and he will likely be dead.

Falric Mislan is torn. Born of a magical Voce and a mundane Dracan, he stands at a crossroads. One direction leads him to the magic he craves, the other to a warriors recognition and status. Stung by his first abortive attempt at awakening his power, Falric throws himself into Dracan life, and inadvertently unearths a perilous talisman.

Watching slip away the last chance of his mother aiding his ambition, Falric accepts that his father's people, and his passing of their Moon Rite, are his only path. But in the aftermath of his find, Falric now faces a bitter enemy who is determined to see him fail.

Spending a month alone in the southern desert for his 'Moon of Solitude' is dangerous enough, but can he survive his own doubts, his unrequited desire for the magic that alludes him…and a man who dreams of deadly vengeance?

Moon Rite is the exhilarating first book in the LGBTQ+ Legend of the Ancients, Books of Locurnia Fantasy series. If you like deep friendship, dangerous trials, and lethal enemies, all with a touch of heated passion, then you'll love this gripping adventure.

ABOUT THE AUTHOR

Born in New Zealand, Deonne grew up on a diet of genie's and witches and space adventure. Not vampires, not then anyway, they were too scary. Back in that day they definitely didn't sparkle.

She spent hours scribbling her version of fanfic in exercise books, on lined refill and coloured notepaper. But then she discovered epic fantasy; Eddings, Kerr, Donaldson & Brooks and felt she had come home.

Later, as happens with most people, she let herself be diverted by the mundanity of adulthood; marriage, widowhood, remarriage, children, separation and even lived through the Christchurch earthquakes, until she remembered the thing she was missing. Thus began her journey into the world of Locurnia.

With family in the queer community and her developing passion for all things MM she decided to marry these two loves together.

You can find her on: -
https://www.facebook.com/deonne.dane/
https://www.facebook.com/groups/KiwiAuthorsRainbowReaders
Or email to: -
deonnedane.author@gmail.com

www.ingramcontent.com/pod-product-compliance
Lightning Source LLC
Chambersburg PA
CBHW020141180626
46810CB00004B/1664